The Child that Haunts Us

The Child that Haunts Us focuses on the symbolic use of the child archetype through the exploration of miniature characters from the realms of children's literature.

Jung argued that the child archetype should never be mistaken for the 'real' child. In this book Susan Hancock considers how the child is portrayed in literature and fairytale and explores the suggestion from Jung and Bachelard that the symbolic resonance of the miniature is inversely proportionate to its size.

We encounter many instances where the miniature characters are a visibly vulnerable 'other', yet often these occur in association with images of the supernatural, as the desired or feared object of adult imagination. In *The Child that Haunts Us* it is emphasised that the treatment by any society, past or present, of its smallest and most vulnerable members is truly revealing of the values it really holds.

This original and sensitive exploration will be of particular interest to undergraduate and postgraduate students as well as academics engaged in Jungian studies, children's literature, childhood studies and those with an interest in socio-cultural constructions of childhood.

Susan Hancock supervises postgraduate students at the National Centre for Research in Children's Literature, Roehampton University, London. She has worked in the field of Children's Literature studies and children's reading for over ten years, having a particular interest in psychoanalytic criticism. A member of the International Association for Jungian Studies, Susan's recent publications relate to Jungian readings of fantasy fiction.

The Child that Haunts Us

Symbols and images in fairytale and miniature literature

Susan Hancock

Routledge
Taylor & Francis Group
LONDON AND NEW YORK

First published 2009
by Routledge
27 Church Road, Hove, East Sussex BN3 2FA

Simultaneously published in the USA and Canada
by Routledge
270 Madison Avenue, New York NY 10016

Routledge is an imprint of the Taylor & Francis Group, an Informa business

Typeset in Times by RefineCatch Limited, Bungay, Suffolk
Printed and bound in Great Britain by TJ International Ltd, Padstow, Cornwall
Paperback cover design by Lisa Dynan
Cover image: Puck, 1841 (oil on canvas) by Dadd, Richard (1817–86). Private Collection/The Bridgeman Art Library.
Nationality/copyright status: English/out of copyright.

This publication has been produced with paper manufactured to strict environmental standards and with pulp derived from sustainable forests.

British Library Cataloguing in Publication Data
A catalogue record for this book is available from the British Library

Library of Congress Cataloging in Publication Data
Hancock, Susan, 1948–
The child that haunts us : symbols and images in fairytale and miniature literature / Susan Hancock.
p. cm.
Includes bibliographical references.
1. Children's literature–Psychological aspects. 2. Fairy tales–Psychological aspects. 3. Children in literature. 4. Archetypes in literature. 5. Jung, C. G. (Carl Gustav), 1875–1961. I. Title.
PN1009.5.P78H36 2009
809′.933523–dc22 2008020286

ISBN: 978–0–415–44775–1 (hbk)
ISBN: 978–0–415–44776–8 (pbk)

To my much loved and long suffering family, Kirsty, Andrew, Caitlin and Jack; my supportive and dearest friends, Carol (my 'twin-sister') and Barry; and last, but never least, my very, very dear husband Peter, who puts up with everything and without whom nothing would be possible.

Contents

Acknowledgements

Grateful thanks are due to colleagues in the National Centre for Research in Children's Literature (NCRCL), the School of Arts, and Roehampton University for enabling me to begin this project with an invaluable period of research leave. My colleagues in the NCRCL, Gillian Lathey, Lisa Sainsbury, Pat Pinsent, Liz Thiel, Alison Waller and Laura Atkins, are due particular thanks for their warm support, as is the NCRCL founder, Kimberley Reynolds. I should also like to thank Tamoko Masaki for her help with regard to the 'Issun-boshi' fairytale, and Yasuko Doi, who located and presented me with a copy of Satoru Sato's book. I should also like to express appreciation to fellow members of the International Association for Jungian Studies for keeping me in touch with Jungian ideas via the passionate discussion list and at exciting conferences. Similarly, I would like to record my appreciation of the opportunity I was given to give voice to preliminary material on 'Thumbelina' at the 2006 Toronto Conference of the Jungian Society for Scholarly Studies. Many thanks are also due to Kate Hawes, Sarah Gibson and Kate Moysen from Routledge, for their invaluable support.

Chapter 1

Introduction

Aspects of 'the child'

In the title and at the heart of my book is an idea, perhaps an entity, that I have called 'the child'. Despite such apparently simple terminology – referring, on the surface, to a human being at a particular stage of development (beyond infancy, but not yet adolescent or adult) – a deeper examination reveals that 'the child' is so very far from a simple term. 'Children' may be represented at any moment in time by 'real' physical bodies, as socio-cultural constructions, as inner memories or echoes of the past or hopes and plans for the future, as the 'other' that is feared or desired or loved or hated by adults who have left the state behind (perhaps) and can now only approach it, warily, from the position of an outsider. Beyond this, as Dewar (1992) and Eekelaar (1991) point out in relation to children's rights, adult–child interaction is itself based upon an acute adult sense of 'difference' and a concomitant perception of the unequal status of children, a perception which may result, at opposite ends of the spectrum, in acts of ultra-protection or in a sense of adult power over a vulnerable child. The socially and culturally defined category of 'childhood' is the broadest category of 'other' which is known to the adult world, and the treatment by any society, past or present, of its smallest and most vulnerable members is truly revealing of the values it really holds.

James, Jenks and Prout (1998) suggest, with some justification, that 'with an intensity perhaps unprecedented, childhood has become popularized, politicized and analysed in a series of interlocking spaces in which the traditional confidence and certainty about childhood and children's social status are being radically undermined' (James et al. 1998: 3). In a postmodern world one may enquire why children should be 'known' with any more certainty than adults 'know' each other or even themselves; nevertheless, parents and other care-givers, educators, legislators and numerous other professionals experience the pressing need and desire to have some understanding of childhood in order to negotiate its space in their lives and within society at any given moment.

Paradoxically, there is an increasing sense of the need to protect children, as vulnerable beings, from predatory adults and a host of influences identified as potentially hostile, but this has gone hand-in-hand with a heightened fear of children. James et al. highlight popular conceptions of a 'lost innocence' and a 'decline in the standards of morality' (James et al. 1998: 52) and a corresponding movement toward increased state control over children's lives. Unlike the situation that pertains when children are the victims of abusive adults, the abduction, torture and murder of 2-year-old James Bulger in 1993 by two 10-year-old children burned upon the public consciousness in Britain conjoint images of 'innocence' and 'evil', visions of the child as sacrificial victim and of the child as demonic perpetrator, images indissolubly linked in a single act (also see the discussion in James et al. 1998: 52). Contemporary images of child soldiers are similarly potent, this time linked in a single body, as the desire to protect and free 'innocent' children from such a fate is aroused, simultaneously, with fear of the idea of a child with a gun.

The potency of such fears is likely to be fostered by a lack of belief in the moral competency of childhood, fuelled, in turn, both by literary images, such as the cruel and murderous child characters of William Golding's *Lord of the Flies* (1954), and by extensive news-media coverage such as that dealing with children and adolescents who turn guns upon classmates and teachers. In an online database detailing 'A Time Line of Recent Worldwide School Shootings' (Information Please® Database, accessed 18 July 2007), twenty-four incidents (1996 to 2006) are listed in which the perpetrator is noted as being a child of 16 years or under (the youngest on the list is 6 years of age). These children are recorded as having shot other students, teachers and/or family members, with forty-three victims catalogued. That such information has been compiled and made available in this way is surely an indication that there is an acute awareness of and interest in children who kill, but there is little to draw readers' attention to the fact that although the database records very real and traumatic events, it also focuses on an incredibly microcosmic proportion of the global child population.

Against such a background it is evident that symbolic and actual are, to no small degree, intertwined in public consciousness, centring on a paradox between a fear *for* and a fear *of* children that has little to do with actual children and everything to do with adult perceptions of the childhood state. At a cultural moment in which sweet and 'cute' images of toddlers throng magazines and television advertisements, and the news media ensure that the public are increasingly aware of the vulnerability of small children, there exist the darker constructions of demonic children in the horror genre of novels and films. Against the babies advertising nappies, toilet paper and washing powders are such books and films as John Wyndham's *Midwich Cuckoos* (1957) and Wolf Rilla's later film version, *The Village of the Damned* (1960), Ira Levin's novel and Roman Polanski's film *Rosemary's Baby* (1968), Richard Donner's and David Selzer's *The Omen* (1976) and John Moore's remake of the latter in 2006 – to name but a few better-known examples. The children depicted in these may be fictional constructs, but real children act out the filmed roles and real writers and directors imaginatively give life to the protagonists that create such a vivid and enduring impact upon audiences.

It would be wrong, however, to think that this is solely a modern-day phenomenon. As Carol Clover suggests, in her book *Men, Women and Chainsaws: Gender in the Modern Horror Movie* (1992), horror stories revisit, constantly, the same basic tale. Even the changelings of folktale and fairytale may well be the precursors of the demonic children mentioned above (and equally, if not more, available to be violently disposed of).

Religious and artistic movements have had a major impact on the ways in which childhood has been viewed in different times and in different groupings within society. Writing in *The Origins and Development of Children's Literature*, Pat Pinsent (2005) speaks to the influence of Calvinism, which, in the late sixteenth and early seventeenth centuries, 'stressed children's potential depravity' (Pinsent 2005: 20) on early writers of 'improving' works for children. Parents were regarded as having a 'responsibility for conveying to children a sense of their sinfulness' (Pinsent 2005: 20, citing the views of Cotton Mather (1663–1728)) and literature of the time, together with later works by Evangelical writers such as Mary Martha Sherwood (1775–1851), bear evidence of such views of childhood. Yet these views could be seen as equating, at some level, with the 'moral' outrage aroused when media reports cite instances of children's behaviour, which is deemed to deviate from constructions of the 'ideal' state in today's society.

Romantic notions of childhood, originating in the Romantic movement in art and literature in the late eighteenth and early nineteenth centuries (exemplified in the works of writers such as Blake, Wordsworth, Coleridge, Byron, Shelley and so on), are, similarly, a construction. These coexisted at times with Evangelical texts but offer a completely opposing perspective on childhood. While the Romantic poet Samuel Taylor Coleridge invokes images of the child as an innocent creature of nature as he tells his slumbering infant: 'But thou, my babe! shalt wander like a breeze/ By lakes and sandy shores, beneath the crags/Of ancient mountain, and beneath the clouds/' in his poem 'Frost at Midnight' (Coleridge 1798/1959: 70), Mary Martha Sherwood's child protagonists (in 'The Story on the Sixth Commandment' from *The History of the Fairchild Family*, 1818) are taken to view the body of a man hanged for fratricide, as a stern warning to reflect on a – comparatively minor – breakfast-time sibling disagreement. In another contrast with Sherwood's tale, Hesba Stretton's child protagonist Jessica (*Jessica's First Prayer*, 1867) is the epitome of uncorrupted innocence surviving in a corrupt environment, and is able to 'save' a more morally suspect adult.

So it can be seen, even in this very brief summary, that from at least as early as the seventeenth century, images of the state of childhood have veered between the divine and the diabolic – children seen as 'gifts from god' or the 'spawn of the devil'. The existence of such a deeply rooted paradox seems to be evidence of a concern with images of 'the child' that, while they may influence ideas on child rearing at any given time, actually only bear lip-service to 'real' children and to the practical issues involved in sharing home and society with those deemed at any given moment to be children.

In *A History of Childhood*, Colin Heywood (2001) summarises current assumptions about the history, not of childhood but of views on childhood, in saying

> there is no essential child for historians to discover, rather . . . commentators have shuffled around a limited repertoire of themes stemming from the biological immaturity of children [he does not, however, engage with what might constitute, definitively, such 'biological immaturity'].
>
> (Heywood 2001: 170)

Indeed, the idea that there might or might not be such an entity to look for is, in itself, supportive of the notion that there is something far beyond the existence of real children at the centre of this debate. If historians cannot resolve the paradox of setting competing views into a linear developmental pattern and sociologists regard all such views as shifting socio-historical constructions, one is driven to ask whether any other mode of thought can move deeper into exploring the need to possess and control a knowledge of childhood and possible origins of the desires and fears surrounding images of 'child' as they arise in adults' minds. Rather than charting competing theories concerning views on the state of childhood it may be more helpful to accept and examine the opposing images of childhood that erupt periodically and to further explore the ways in which such imaginings become entangled with the 'real' world of living, breathing, human children.

Taking a step back and attempting to view this maelstrom of competing ideas from a distance, it seems that in talking about 'the child', regardless of the type of discourse, the debate is, more often than not, less about children per se, but (whether explicitly or implicitly) about the relationships the child is deemed to be a part of or enveloped within. At one level there is the idea of the child in some form of familial bond: mother–child; father–child; sibling–sibling (whether that relationship is biological or circumstantial). At another there is the child in some form of relationship with wider society: authority-figure–child (whether the authority-figure is constituted as a rule enforcer, for example a representative of the police, or a guardian of welfare, for example social worker or educator); adult–child (in any encounter); peer–child (friend or foe).

At a deeper and more abstract level, there is also the possible relationship between an adult subject and an 'inner child' posited in books such as Jeremiah Abrams' (1991) *Reclaiming the Inner Child*. Here Abrams, in his introduction, speaks to appearances of images of an inner child, not only arising in personal dreams, but also given form in art, literature and myths, as a positive and vibrant symbol of eternal, ever-self-renewing life and vigour. While I would hesitate over the overwhelmingly positive tone of Abrams' words (where is the negative side of this wonder child? – but more of this in later chapters) there seems to be much to suggest, as I will expand upon in the next section, that the human unconscious does give rise to images of what Carl Gustav Jung (1875–1961) terms the 'child archetype', as discussed in some depth in his essay (1939–40) 'The

Psychology of the Child Archetype' (published in *Essays on a Science of Mythology*).

It seems to me, and this is the guiding impulse at the root of my book, that there is one area of discourse in which one can begin to see all the ways in which the adult world imaginatively constructs adult–child relationships, whether familial, social, cultural or inner, and that is the area of children's literature, where adult writers frequently create child characters in such relationships. In particular, narrative fantasy fictions allow writers free reign to the impulse to create complex images *entangling* the attempted child-in-the-world re-creation with the symbolic content posited by the idea of the inner child. It is therefore my intention to examine certain texts from the realms of fantasy fiction for children (a more detailed rationale follows later) with the aim of discovering both what their adult creators say (consciously and unconsciously) *about* the children (and their relationships) imaginatively constructed in their fictions and *to* the children who encounter such fictions as young readers.

Jungian psychoanalytic criticism as it may be applied to fantasy children's literature

In my view, the ideal tool with which to explore the symbolic subtext of images of children in narrative fantasy fictions is psychoanalytic criticism. My aim is not, however, to use a Freudian approach, but rather to focus upon the insights that may be offered by Jungian psychoanalytic criticism and more recent developments in the field of Jungian literary theory (see, for example, Rowland 1999; Baumlin et al. 2004) and post-Jungian thought. My reasons align with Brian Attebery's insightful comment in *Strategies of Fantasy*: 'Whereas Freud looks to origins, Jung looks to ends: not where we came from but what we may grow into' (Attebery 1992: 30).

There has been much public interest in Freudian ideas and in Freudian psychoanalytical criticism, perhaps symbolised in popular consciousness by images such as the phallus, the sexualised infant and the Oedipus complex on the one hand, and the ego, superego and id on the other (the latter even featuring, metaphorically, in Fred Wilcox's fascinating science fiction film *Forbidden Planet*, 1956). While this is a wildly oversimplistic summary of a major body of thought, nevertheless it is probably true to say that when Freudian theory focuses on the infant and child, it is, predominantly, in the manner of looking back to these stages as the source of later neuroses. Interest centres upon a developmental awareness of infants and children as inevitably incomplete adults-in-the-making rather than engaging with the *idea* of child – together with its futurity – in the form of the child motif.

Jung was a complex thinker, whose insights derived from widely differing sources: his own practical work as an assistant doctor working for the psychiatrist Eugen Bleuler; his lifelong involvement with spiritualism; his extensive scholarship in the fields of comparative religion and mythology; a fascination with alchemy and its metaphorical potential; and, perhaps most significantly, his sustained period of self-analysis (see, for example, Rowland 2002: 1–22). In his writings, Jung puts forward, persuasively, a model of the psyche which comprises both conscious and unconscious levels, the latter being further layered into the personal unconscious and a deeper, non-personal and inborn layer (inherited in terms of humankind rather than a personal family inheritance) which he terms the *collective unconscious* (see, for example, discussion of this in 'The Personal and the Collective Unconscious' in *CW* 7 and in 'Archetypes of the Collective Unconscious' in *CW* 9i). It is his ideas on the collective unconscious, and the *archetypes* (see below) he sees as arising there that are particularly helpful for this study.

Susan Rowland (2002) sets out, with exceptional clarity, key areas of Jungian theory in *Jung: A Feminist Revision*. Having discussed Jungian ideas of the unconscious she asks, 'what does it mean to say that the unconscious is a source of healing and value in human life?' (Rowland 2002: 29). Her answer is of great importance to a study that follows images of the child motif, and surrounding figures from fairytale into literary creations:

> the unconscious contains inherited potential structures called archetypes. As a result, Jung's unconscious is collective because all people inherit more or less the same archetypes as basic substances. I have referred to archetypes very carefully as 'potential structures' and 'substances', because there is a common misconception that Jung's archetypes are inherited images. This is not true. An archetype is an inborn potential for a certain sort of image. What the mental image will look like will not only depend upon the collective unconscious. Archetypal images also reflect the conscious experiences of the person as a subject in history, culture and time.
>
> (Rowland 2002: 29)

In a previous exploration of children's literature (Hancock 2005), using Jungian theory, I have found it useful to draw attention (when looking at child and adolescent characters) to those archetypes identified by Jung as the anima, animus, child, shadow and trickster. Drawing on Jung's ideas, particularly as expressed in 'Archetypes of the Collective Unconscious' (*CW* 9i), I have put together a table giving a very brief, preliminary indication of my interpretation of the meanings of the terms Jung uses (see Table 1).

Also of importance, but this time in considering the relationships in which child characters occur, are archetypal images of the mother, wise old woman and wise old man. Drawing on Jung's ideas regarding the first of these (see discussion of the 'Psychological Aspects of the Mother Archetype': *CW* 9i) it is clear to see a diversity of images of the Mother (or *Great Mother*). There are positive and negative polarities, given form in ideas such as the madonna versus the whore of western Christianity, and the different aspects of the Hindu goddess Sakti – Durga 'perceived in Northern India as the gentle bride' (Jordan 1992: 66) and the 'terrible and malignant' Kali (Jordan 1992: 126). Similarly, in fairytales, the 'good' mother and the witch may both appear, and the terrifying stepmother (sometimes mother) may arise to persecute the children in her care (see, for example, the Grimm Brothers' (1812) versions of the 'Cinderella' and 'Snow White' stories and books by modern-day picturebook artists, such as Anthony Browne, who intimates through his artwork that the mother and witch in his picturebook *Hansel and Gretel* (1981) are one and the same). In similar vein, the wise old woman may appear in benevolent or malign aspect, perhaps epitomised in the 'thirteen wise women' of the Grimms' 'Brier Rose' tale (Grimm Brothers, trans. Zipes 1992: 186), in which twelve are beneficent gift-givers and one is malevolent and vengeful (in later retellings, these often feature as twelve fairy godmothers and one evil witch).

If the anima is, by virtue of name, the soul-image, Jung identifies the archetype he names the *wise old man* as the archetype of the spirit. Referring to the dream of a theological student, Jung comments on the appearance within the dream of images of a black-robed white magician and a white-robed black magician. He suggests that the two may be interpreted as images of the bipolar aspects of the wise old man and advises that the archetype frequently arises in dreams and fantasies in the image of a guru, magician, teacher or other similar 'superior' figure (see discussion in 'The Phenomenology of the Spirit in Fairytales': *CW* 9i: 398–9) who

Table 1 Key archetypes: a brief interpretation of Jung's terms

Anima	Frieda Fordham glosses this as 'the unconscious feminine side of a man' (Fordham 1953: 122). According to Jung's extensive writings about the *anima* (or soul-image) it seems that it may appear in a man's unconscious as anything from an angel to a demonic being. It is the experience of 'otherness', the alternate to the male ego, which frequently takes imaginative form as a woman and may be projected onto a living woman (see *CW* 9i, paras 52–66 and elsewhere).
Animus	The equivalent figure which is said to arise as 'masculine' in women. Perhaps unsurprisingly (being a man, and thus not speaking to any encounter with this figure *within* his own psyche) Jung does not enlarge on the *animus* to any great degree and the tone used is quite dismissive, emphasising the negative potential of the figure.
Child	The child archetype may appear in divine or monstrous form. Jung advises that it can symbolise both past and future, emphasising that the child motif does not arise from a real child and associating the motif with ideas of rebirth (miraculous birth). In Jung's words: 'The "child" is all that is abandoned and exposed and at the same time divinely powerful' (Jung in Jung and Kerényi 1963: 98).
Shadow	Andrew Samuels summarises this helpfully in advising that 'the *shadow* [is] a word coined by Jung to sum up what each man fears and despises and cannot accept in himself' (Samuels 1986: 31).
Trickster	The archetypal trickster figure is widely acknowledged beyond the bounds of Jungian psychoanalytic criticism. Examples abound in myth and folktale, from Ghana's Ashanti Spider God and his West Indian counterpart, Anancy Spiderman (see Berry 1988), to Loki of Norse mythology and the coyote, raven (and other) figures in native American myths (see Scott Littleton 2002: 508–11). Linked to carnival, the trickster arises as 'an unreflective joker, shape-shifter and (false) saviour, with a dual nature, bestial and divine' (Hancock 2005: 45).

is 'paradoxically sometimes seen as father, sometimes son of the anima' (Hancock 2005: 45).

In aligning discussion of archetypes with literary theory, however, there is always a danger that this can degenerate into something of a 'spot the archetype' game. This can be a reductive and sterile practice, one which implies that archetypes survive, trans-culturally and trans-temporally, as intact expressions of some essential and in some way 'knowable' unconscious that arise, quite unproblematically, in artistic productions. Rowland (2004), in setting out the post-Jungian development of a Jungian literary theory, draws attention to Jung's view of the 'human psyche' as 'a mythmaking organ that needs to creatively engage with the "other" through such cultural practices as fairytales, religion or art' (Rowland 2004). She suggests that 'a work of art for Jung is a kind of condensed material moment in which a culture is thinking consciously and unconsciously, together' (Rowland 2004). Here the idea of a creative engagement with 'other', drawing together collective unconscious content and culturally sited conscious and unconscious activity, promises that both fairytales and artistic creations have immense potential to suggest insights to those who seek to engage with the archetypal images they express in ways other than reductive 'identificatory' studies. Indeed, James and Tita Baumlin (in *Post-Jungian Criticism: Theory and Practice*) regard it as self-evident that the cultural and historical moment is inevitably entangled in any creative imagining of archetypal content, stating: 'we take it as a given that a literary text's archetypal images are shaped by history and culture' (Baumlin et al. 2004: 118).

Returning focus to images of the child archetype, in Jungian thought the 'child' (as referred to in Table 1) is detached from ideas of living, breathing children and arises as an imagining of collective unconscious content, capable of surfacing at any point in an individual's life, or, collectively, in any culture or society. Thus the idea of 'child' is never wholly in the past for an adult, but may arise at any time. Jung particularly warns against the kind of thinking that identifies the symbolic idea of 'child' with actual living, breathing children, emphasising that:

> the mythological idea of the child is emphatically not a copy of the empirical child but a *symbol* clearly recognizable as such: it is a wonder-child, a divine child, begotten, born, and brought up in quite extraordinary circumstances, and not – this is the point – a human child. . . . Moreover the mythological 'child' has various forms: now a god, giant, Tom Thumb, animal, etc., and this points to a causality that is anything but rational or concretely human.
>
> (Jung in Jung and Kerényi 1963: 80n)

That is not to say, however, as I have suggested earlier, that this does not have the potential to become confused with, entwined with, relationships with living, breathing children, particularly when images of the child motif arise in literature for children. Fictions created for (or deemed suitable for) a child audience are complex sites of adult–child negotiation. When fiction is composed for children, or drawn into the domain from fairytale origins, or simply read by or to children, it can be seen as a space where adult and child meet, where hopes and fears for the future are located and where adult-created images of childhood can be exposed. Here living, breathing children may encounter a writer's simulation of a living, breathing child inextricably interwoven with the metaphorical form of that writer's imagining of collective archetypal content. Drawing on ideas from Rowland's persuasive presentation of the possibility of 'A Jungian Reader Theory' (1999: 60–83) it can be seen that the living, breathing children that are the implied readers of children's literature are not the least significant part of this complicated and nested child–adult–child entanglement. As Rowland (1999) concludes:

> Reader-response theory states that the meaning of a literary work is not locked away in the text but inheres in the creative engagement between text and reader. It goes further to suggest that reading reformulates the reader's subjectivity, particularly through liberating some unconscious forces. . . . Reading a fiction will provoke mental images and these will be affected by the Jungian unconscious.
>
> (Rowland 1999: 196)

Overall, the children's literature domain is a multi-genre province of thought. It has boundaries which stretch far wider than discrete textual units, drawing in picture narratives, numerous narratives with shared or even invisible authorship and characters that frequently traverse textual boundaries, appearing as play artefacts and as the heroes (female and male) of multiple plots in varied mediums. The children's literature domain inevitably looks *back* towards its writers' imagined childhood selves and *forward* to the adults its readers will become – adults of the future still carrying the legacy of their childhood selves and thus perpetuating an endless cycle of child within adult within child. But, at a collective level, the fairytales that so often find themselves drawn into this seething site of adult–child engagement carry even deeper symbolic content. Jung is careful to distinguish between the collective underlying propensity to give image to archetypes and the form that these may take, and it is this variance between images that emerge through a writer's personal, cultural and socio-historical context that may be so revealing of writer and times (see, for example, discussion of myth and fairytale in 'Archetypes of the Collective Unconscious' (*CW* 9i: 6)) and so significant for the child–reader–text engagement.

In this study, it is my intention to look at images given to the child motif in fairytale and myth and to look at a possible evolution from these forms into complex characters which include both symbolic content and the simulated-child protagonists of later fictions composed by adults, specifically (at least ostensibly) for child readers. My particular focus will be on the relationships that are depicted between these child forms and the adults they encounter. In this way, I hope to point to the arising of possible underlying unconscious content and to compare the forms that are given to this by different individuals in differing places and times. My stated intention is to use, as a tool, psychoanalytic criticism based around Jungian theory. There will be times, however, when it seems useful and appropriate to draw upon post-Jungian modifications to, and developments of, Jung's ideas. In this I shall be guided, in particular, by Samuels' (1986) invaluable discussion of post-Jungian developments in *Jung and the Post-Jungians*, by Rowland's (1999) influential *C.G. Jung and Literary Theory: The Challenge from Fiction*, and by the authors of the collected essays in *Post-Jungian Criticism: Theory and Practice*, edited by James S. Baumlin, Tita French Baumlin and George H. Jenson (though I absolve all from any misuse I may make of their ideas through any misunderstandings of my own!). This is intended to be a pragmatic study, so I make no apology for making use of whatever I feel adds insight to the readings that follow.

'The child' in children's literature

As examples earlier in this introduction indicate, the ways in which 'the child' is represented in fictions produced for living, breathing children's consumption can be a useful indicator of both public and personal thoughts concerning the outer visible child, symbolic and actual, and the child motif as it arises from the unconscious, in dreams and fantasies. Unquestionably, at the heart of the majority of children's literature is the child-in-the-world topic, an exploration of the ways in which children encounter the world and how they are perceived as learning to live and form relationships within it. However, since children's literature is generally created by adults, it is inevitably peopled with surrogate-child protagonists, constructions that represent adult text-creators' ideas of what a child 'is', shaded by their own cultural, personal and social contexts. As Peter Hollindale (1997) suggests, in his examination of *Signs of Childness in Children's Books*: 'The author must *construct childhood* from an amalgam of personal retrospect, acquaintance with contemporary children, and *an acquired system of beliefs as to what children are, and should be, like*' (Hollindale 1997: 12, my emphases).

The absence of living, breathing children from the processes associated with the creation and production of children's literature has been well documented (see, for example, Rose 1984; Lesnik-Oberstein 1994; Hollindale 1997). It is a sense of the 'otherness' of the idea of 'child' (see my introductory discussion) that underlies the processes of character creation in children's literature, so that child protagonists, laden with a burden of adults' fears, hopes, assumptions and desires, arise textually within the children's literature domain as a jigsaw puzzle of disparate elements. There is the adult text-creator's idea of childness,[1] in essence what he or she believes a child could or should be, plus a form that is thought to be attractive to child readers – a toy, another child, an animal perhaps. There may also be elements of extra-textual proto-characters: 'floating' metaphorical representations of archetypal propensities liberated from pre-texts,[2] such as the vividly created 'eternal child' passed on from J. M. Barrie's enduring 'Peter Pan' creation. (There are innumerable versions of this proto-character, first called into being by J. M. Barrie as the protagonist in a story within a story for adults, *The Little White Bird* (1902), and endlessly re-created, to this day, in multimedia retellings – picturebooks, television cartoons, films and the like.) More complex characters have simulated child-psyches attached to such archetypal imaginings, as their creators strive to convince their audiences that these are believable children, with thoughts and emotions that child readers can recognise and possibly identify with.[3] Characters can also be given distancing disguises, as animals, machines, alien forms and the like, protecting child readers from seeing themselves as the adult world may see them. Yet that very disguise (and the perceived need for it) is revealing of adult attitudes toward children.

Jung points to the endlessly re-created images of archetypes that arise in myths and fairytales in 'The Phenomenology of the

Spirit in Fairytales' (for example, *CW* 9i: 400). If this is accepted, readings of such texts from a Jungian perspective have the potential to reveal the deep underlying concerns of the eras and minds in which such narratives develop or are transferred to the domain. Fairytales and other fantasy texts for children in which the presence of archetypal images of the 'child' may be discerned are of special interest: freed to a certain extent from overt 'realities', they are, nevertheless, products of adult storytellers' minds, filled, through the medium of their fictional protagonists, by an engagement with the 'idea' of child that may be composed of both conscious and unconscious content. As in all areas where adults are drawn to engage with the childhood condition these fictions are potentially sites of immense symbolic significance (see, for example, *CW* 9i: 275).

The child archetype, as discussed in Jung's essay 'The Psychology of the Child Archetype' (in *Essays on a Science of Mythology*), is a fascinating and recurrent motif in myth and fairytale. Jung links it with healing and the movement to psychic wholeness, suggesting that the 'child motif represents the preconscious, childhood aspect of the collective psyche', but that, perhaps paradoxically, it 'is potential future' (Jung in Jung and Kerényi 1963: 80, 83). In this study I shall be investigating what may be learned from examining moments the motif enters imaginal form as a character in fairytale, or quasi-fairytale (such as the 'Peter Pan' story) and its later appearances as part of more complex character formations in narratives composed specifically for an audience of human children.

The children portrayed in literary narratives, however much they are disguised in order to appear to readers as 'real' people, are distanced from their human counterparts. In looking at literary narratives for children, I am acutely aware of the distinctions between archetype, archetypal image, character and simulated human being and not suggesting that there is an actual link between living, breathing children and appearances of the motif; I do believe, however, that appearances of the motif in the children's literature domain potentially have great significance. As I have previously noted (Hancock 1999), children's literature is deeply implicated, at both an individual and a social level, in the potential absorption by child readers of what it may mean to be a child. Specifically, what it may mean to be a child born in a specific time and place and encountering the adult world of that 'chrono-topical moment'. (I am hereafter using 'chrono-topical moment' as a portmanteau term to signify an amalgam of influences of time and place – both time and place being understood to incorporate social, cultural and physical influences.)[4] Children, as readers, are likely to imbibe from fictions produced for them at least some of the ethical and social beliefs and systems propagated by the surrounding dominant, and initially alien, adult community. Where adult writers give image to the child motif and set it into a literature which they intend to speak to an audience composed, at least partly, of children then its usage becomes particularly revealing as the potency of the symbol is mixed with an individual adult writer's imaging of collective and personal content for a child audience.

Before narrowing focus to explore specific narratives, it is useful to look more generally at the interrelationships between archetypal images and the characters of fairytale and literary creations for children.[5] The creation of characters within literary narratives is, in itself, closely interwoven with the archetypal imaging propensity within the human psyche. James Hillman, one of the chief exponents of the post-Jungian Archetypal School of analytical psychology (see Samuels 1986: 241–8), speaks to Jung's recognition of the significance of the character side of the plot–character interaction inherent in all narrative and compares this with the limitations of Freud's monomythic focus on plot (Hillman 1983: 9–10). In choosing to use a predominantly Jungian approach to my exploration of the child motif I have been influenced by this distinction, since the Jungian focus, in aligning with my studies of character formation in the domain of literature for children (Hancock 1999), seems the more fruitful for this purpose.

Yet, whichever predominates, plot and character are inevitably linked in narrative, so that it could be said that myths and the earliest fairytales – although it is very difficult to isolate truly 'original' forms – give metaphorical life to archetypal plots for archetypal figures to enact, drawing out the possibilities that are the latent potential within them. But, later, when archetypal characters and plots are drawn into literary narratives for children, I want to explore the further complications that occur in the metamorphosis of archetypal images, into forms that are mingled with the chrono-topically specific, conscious creations of individual writers, examining the choices surrounding such occurrences and what they reveal of the times, cultures and the varying writer and reader contexts in which they occur.

Jungian interpretations of literature can offer invaluable insights into what Jung calls the *time-spirit* (*CW* 9i: 386) of any chrono-topical moment. Through an awareness of this, readers can become sensitive to the mood of a time or culture – seeing the images and situations that are created by its writers as an ongoing engagement between an inner and outer life. As Inez Martinez (2004: 105) suggests, in her essay 'Reading for Psyche: Kate Chopin's *The Awakening*', '[i]maginative literature is to the collective as dreams are to the dreamer', proposing 'that a fundamental purpose of literary analysis is comparable to that of dream analysis: the understanding of psyche, both personal and collective' (Martinez 2004: 105).

During the move into narrative, whether fairytales or stories designed for and aimed at child readers, the forms that are given to archetypal material can become more complex. In the first instance, fairytale imaginings of archetypes frequently place these in alliances which may be 'conjoint' (within one character) or 'partnered' (with plot actions/situations mediated by a partner or partners). They may also be split in aspect between the dualities of the 'good' and shadow sides. It is these aspects that I shall be looking at in Part I of this work, in the chapters which look at stories about the characters Tom Thumb, Issun-boshi, Tömmelise and Mopsa. Table 2 shows how such alliances may appear within a narrative in which a character may be read as a metaphorical manifestation of the child archetype.

Of particular interest is the conjoining of child archetype and hero, since it is suggested that pre-adolescent, independent child readers frequently 'focus [in their reading of fiction] on issues of identity, in the image of the powerful or clever hero or heroine who in one guise or another is the principal archetype of most stories school-age children read' (Appleyard 1994: 59). Fairytales provide metaphorical forms of such archetypal propensities (both female and male) in narrative form, but many literary texts written and marketed for children move beyond this and draw on a dual legacy. On the one hand there are archetypal images, the symbolic 'character-content' of fairytale, legend and myth, regarded by some as suitable, even essential, fare for children (see Bettelheim's (1978) controversial work *The Uses of Enchantment*). On the other hand the dominant mode employed in forming characters in novels for children is that of 'classic realism', in which writers attempt to create simulacra of psychologically coherent 'possible' people. Jacqueline Rose (1984) warns of

> the remarkable consistency with which one particular aesthetic is being laid on the child and associated with children. It is an aesthetic which takes its reference from the nineteenth-century

Table 2 Appearances of the child motif

Appearances of the child motif	*Situations and external alliances (plot in narrative terms)*	*Modes and conjoined alliances (character in narrative terms)*	*Tropically represented aspects of 'child' motif (metaphor in literary terms)*
Affirming powerlessness	In the situation of a victim: abandoned or lost and suffering		Miniature (metaphorical-child)
Yet paradoxically empowered		Divine-child or evil-child (shadow) with supernatural powers	Giant (hyperbolic-child)
Alliances with other archetypal figures (1) conjoint		The child archetype may be conjoined with the trickster, hero, anima or animus	
(2) partnered	Linked to parental and other authority figures, e.g. wise old man or woman		

> novel . . . which measure the success of a book according to its ability to convince us that it is no such thing.
>
> (Rose 1984: 61–2)

Maria Nikolajeva (2004) suggests that there is an audience-age-related movement within fiction away from archetype toward attempted psychological realism: 'the movement from hero to character, from vehicles of certain actions necessary for the plot toward fully developed psychological portraits' (Nikolajeva 2004: 174). However, this may be less of a movement *from* one to the other, and rather more a spectrum of characterisation in which an archetypal, and thus metaphorical, core image is increasingly overlaid with the mimetic representation of a 'real' person.

Effectively, within the children's literature domain, there is frequently an elision of metaphorical content with apparent psychological realism in the 'classic realist' sense. If, as Appleyard suggests, 'the distinctive role readers take at this stage is to imagine themselves as heroes and heroines of romances that are unconscious analogues of their own lives' (Appleyard 1994: 59–60), such dual ancestry in character formation is highly significant, in that it presents to children, at a stage during which they are particularly likely to respond by immersing themselves in the hero role, something that may well be apparently 'real' yet effectively symbolic. The latter part, submerged as subtext underneath the alluring construction of 'classic realist' character, is still capable of speaking at the deepest level to child (and adult) readers. Thus the archetypal significance remains and may, in turn, spark images from the unconscious of the reader who has made a direct and conscious investment in the apparently 'living' character.

Rowland (1999), in linking Wolfgang Iser's views (as set out in *The Act of Reading*, 1978) of reader-response theories with Jungian ideas on 'active imagination', speaks to Iser's contention that 'reading is a form of enlarging of subjectivity by providing structures by which the unconscious can influence ideation, provoke and shape images so constructing the subjectivity of the reader anew' (Rowland 1999: 63). She argues that:

> Iser quotes Freud to support his view that reading liberates some unconscious forces from repression to become ingredients of an evolving consciousness in the act of reading. ['Iser refers to Freud, pp.158ff'] Yet if we substitute a Jungian definition of the archetypal unconscious (as inherently meaningful) for Freud's, Iser could be said to have described reading fiction as a form of 'active imagination' ['Jung's therapeutic method of using an image as a stimulus for the patient to fantasise upon'] whereby reading provokes the unconscious shaping of subjectivity which Jung called 'individuation'.
>
> (Rowland 1999: 63)

So it may well be that the whole – writer's metaphorical imagining of archetypal content, writer's simulated child, and child reader's stimulated imagining of archetypal content and engagement with the simulated child – can become an alliance of adult interest in forming the minds of, or speaking to, child readers; adult interest in the commercial aspects of potential child audiences; and of deeper and more unconscious content brought into imaginative life by both (adult) writer and (child) reader. Since this complex amalgam is frequently presented to readers who are negotiating their own identities through imaginal immersion in others, there needs to be an awareness of the phenomenon. Given, too, that children's literature is currently a favourite repository of the notion of a 'classic' cannon of works, appropriate and valuable for child readers of *all* places and all times, it is important to recognise that the desires and fears of any culture may be learned about and, at a more unconscious level, absorbed from the ways its writers imagine the fictional characters they present to those in whom its futures are invested.

Miniature characters and worlds

Nowhere can the process described above be seen more clearly than in miniature literature (that is, the literature domain featuring miniature characters and worlds), where surrogate-child characters, distanced from child readers by their abnormally small size, are made available for an engagement with issues surrounding their exaggerated vulnerability in the face of full-sized objects. Indeed, writing in *The Poetics of Space*, Bachelard (1964) suggests that:

> The cleverer I am at miniaturizing the world, the better I possess it. But in doing this, it must be understood that values become condensed and enriched in miniature . . . miniature literature – that is to say, the aggregate of literary images that are commentaries on inversions in the perspective of size – stimulates profound values.
>
> (Bachelard 1964: 150)

Importantly, miniature characters, such as the Tom Thumb and Thumbelina types, can be seen to function as vivid visual metaphors for the adult-perceived vulnerability of children. Effectively each miniature literature text, at some point, addresses the same issue – the inequality generated by the size-differential between its miniature characters and the full-size worlds that surround them. Yet the responses of characters such as Tom Thumb and Thumbelina, for example, differ widely, both from each other and, sometimes, even in relation to different versions of stories carrying the character's name. The multiplicity of ways which text-creators find to resolve this inequality are thus able to contribute to a domain-wide dialogue, one which is vitally concerned with adult-constructions of living, breathing children's places in the 'known possible world';[6] an ongoing dialogue taking place in the domain over space and time. Miniature beings thus occupy the ultimate child-position, visibly separated from the adult world as a vulnerable 'other', yet often in 'suspect' association with images of the supernatural in fairy form (here I am using the term 'fairy' to encompass the full range of miniature supernatural beings, from elves to goblins and the more hominiform fairy tribes) as the feared or desired object of adult imagination.

One of the practical difficulties to be overcome in choosing case studies to illuminate any specific aspect of children's literature is the sheer volume of published material from which to choose. To draw together, in this book, both fairytale characters and comparable characters in literary narratives for children, it is necessary to find some common ground upon which to base the choice of case studies which follow. However, as I have already suggested, it is not simply necessity that has led me to the choice of miniature literature, I have been led by many considerations, including Jung's comment that 'the mythological child has various forms: now a god, giant, *Tom Thumb*, animal etc.' (Jung in Jung and Kerényi 1963: 80n, my emphasis).

The miniature has a well-established place in folklore. In his study of *The Folktale*, Stith Thompson (1946) suggests:

> In ancient literature we frequently hear of impossibly small men and this theme has retained its popularity, not only in the literary account of the travels of Lemuel Gulliver, but also in the widely told popular story of *Tom Thumb* (Type 700).[7]
>
> (Thompson 1946: 86)

Thompson is of the view that the latter tale 'would seem to be a story whose history would repay a thorough investigation such as it has never received' (Thompson 1946: 87). He suggests that occurrences of the 'Tom Thumb' story are widespread:

> A glance at its distribution indicates that it is a European story, well established over the whole continent, which has been carried to the nearer parts of Asia, to scattered points in Africa and the Cape Verde Islands, and thence to Jamaica, the Bahamas, the American Negroes of the southern states, and to one tribe of Indians in the Plains.
>
> (Thompson 1946: 86)

Kerényi too, in his essay 'The Primordial Child in Primordial Times' (companion to Jung's 'The Psychology of the Child Archetype'), refers to miniature embodiments of the child motif, as in his recounting of Finnish legend: 'A man rose out of the sea, a hero from the waves. He was not the hugest of huge nor yet the smallest of small: he was as big as a man's thumb, the span of a woman' (Kerényi in Jung and Kerényi 1963: 41).

Just as the children's literature domain is a polymorphous place, with multiple manifestations of expression, including picture books and illustrated novels; books of poetry and rhyme; short stories; comics and graphic novels; television cartoons; acted drama and animated film, so too is miniature literature. The latter shares with children's literature a tendency toward varied authorship, with joint ventures (particularly in the area of picture narratives); anonymous offerings; oral tales and retellings; and the conventional single-author 'ownership' of texts that is more familiar in narratives offered to an adult audience. Coupled with Jung's assertion (see earlier) that a 'Tom Thumb' is a common manifestation of the child archetype, the way is clearly pointed toward the validity of using miniature literature as the source for both fairytale case studies *and* for texts in which to explore the significance of instances of the child archetype as it occurs in literary character formation within children's literature.

The miniature character at the heart of miniature literature is in itself an intriguing phenomenon, one which has endured through time and space, appearing in folktales and literary productions from diverse societies and eras and breaking through discrete textual boundaries. Iona and Peter Opie (1974) comment:

> Tom Thumb has . . . remained a favourite character in English legendary lore; and his counterparts in Continental Europe such as *Le petit Poucet* in France . . .; *Daumesdick, Däumling*, and *Daumerling* . . . in Germany; and *Svend Tomling*, in Denmark, . . . also have long histories. Further afield, the English imp may be compared with *Vamuna* in India and *Issun Boshi* ('Little One Inch') in Japan.
>
> (Opie and Opie 1974: 31–2)

My own researches also highlight the enduring and wide-ranging nature of the literary miniature. Miniature literature rhyme and poetry narratives have been created across centuries. There are, for example, rhyme versions of the 'Tom Thumb' story, such as the one reproduced by John Ashton in 1882 and attributed to Wright (1700), and narrative poems such as Christina Rossetti's *Goblin Market* (written in 1859 and published in 1862). The latter is an interestingly ambivalent text which has versions in poetry collections for both adult and child readers and has also given impetus to numerous picture versions, ranging from Dante Gabriel Rossetti's early contribution in 1862 to his sister's work to Arthur Rackham's celebrated revisioning of the tale in 1933. They have also been created across the globe. Palmer Cox's 'Brownies' texts, such as *The Brownies: Their Book* (1888), which contain both rhymes and pictures by Cox, are part of the American 'miniature' heritage, while *The Witch and the Mischievous Seven* (Mitgutsch 1985) was originally published in Germany as *Der Hexe und die Seben Fexe* in 1970. The latter is a rhyme and picture book about 'Frixes': 'spindly little people who are full of fun' (trans. Marsh 1985, page preceding title page) and their 'shadow' counterparts, the witch's 'wicked little imp[s]' (front endpaper). Here the pictorially envisioned miniature characters are created by Ali Mitgutsch, and have verbally constructed forms brought into being by Irmgard Hailer and re-created in English by Gwen Marsh. Picture narratives, such as Raymond Briggs' *The Man* (1992), which portray miniature characters, are too numerous to begin to catalogue, since almost all verbal-miniature-literature texts include picture images of the miniature protagonists, often in multiple versions over time and between geographical locations.

Novels about miniature characters written during the latter half of the twentieth century frequently occur in series, demonstrating the extent to which the characters predominate over particular episodic plots. There are, for example, Mary Norton's 'borrowers',[8] who are depicted in books, films and on video as being '[f]ive or six inches [tall]' (Norton 1983: 10) and exist at the nexus of fantasy and realism in their very conventional (though unbelievably tiny) family unit (see Part II) and Terry Pratchett's 'Nomes', who are to be found in a trilogy of written texts (1989–90) and also on video. Lynne Reid Banks has created the 'Indian in the Cupboard' series, featuring the adventures of two boys and their 'living' miniature toys (Banks 1981–93); these, similarly, appear in both written and filmed narratives. There are also many single texts which, nevertheless, link to other texts and writers across time, including Pauline Clarke's *The Twelve and the Genii* (1962), the story of a young boy and his discovery that the Brontë family's toy soldiers, heroes of the Brontë children's early fictional tales, are 'really' miniature living beings, and Helen Cresswell's *Polly Thumb* (1994), with its echoes (soon subverted) of Andersen's 'Tömmelise', about a young girl who magically shrinks to the size of a thumb. There is even a miniature ghost in Mary Hoffman's *The Second-hand Ghost* (1986): 'a figure appeared of a man in rather baggy trousers and rumpled jacket, with a cap on his head. Only it had no colour and Lisa could still see her hairbrush and china rabbit showing straight through it. Also it was about three and a half inches tall' (Hoffman 1986: 11).

Again, as with texts in picture and rhyme, miniature literature available in novel form in the UK also includes translations of foreign-language narratives such as Selma Lagerlöf's *The Wonderful Adventures of Nils*, about a boy, transformed by an elf into 'a little, little creature' (1950: 8) (originally published in Swedish, in two parts, in 1906 and 1907, see Part II), Erich Kästner's *The Little Man* (first published as *Der Kleine Mann* in 1963, see Part II) and Satoru Sato's *A Little Country No One Knows* (1988) (first published as *Daremo shiranai chiisa na kuni* in 1959, see Part II). Sato's text, located in wartime and post-war Japan, features the Korobokkuru – a race of elf-like people each smaller than a child's little finger. Miniature characters also feature in texts from the 'New World' with races of primeval miniatures such as the trickster-allied 'Nyols' in Patricia Wrightson's *An Older Kind of Magic* (1972) and *The Nargun and the Stars* (1973), the gnomes in Upton Sinclair's *The Gnomobile* (1936) and characters such as E. B. White's anthropomorphic mouse-child *Stuart Little* (1945).

Earlier British fairytale-style novels featuring miniature characters include: Charles Kingsley's *Water-Babies* (1863), Jean Ingelow's *Mopsa the Fairy* (1869, see Part I), George MacDonald's *The Princess and the Goblin* (1872) and *Little Grey Men* by 'BB' (1942, see Part II). There are also innumerable other texts featuring fairies, pixies, brownies and the like, emanating from a multiplicity of times and places and in a variety of mediums. For example, in addition to the many film and animated versions of the 'Tom Thumb' story, with source material taken from both English and European folktale collections, and of the 'Thumbelina' story, there are interesting films such as *Willow* (1988), in which a midget, with help from minute brownies and full-size humans, rescues a human baby.

The characters of miniature literature even creep into fictional narratives for adults – an interesting contrast – as, for example, in the Victorian fairy painting genre, that 'particularly British phenomenon which flourished between the 1790s and the 1870s' (Phillpotts

1978: 4). Paintings such as Richard Dadd's *Puck* (first exhibited in 1841) show vividly the shadow side of such images (see cover): here a sinister and palely naked baby figure is captured for adult voyeuristic gaze in an internal frame within the painting. A demonic quasi-child, he is depicted controlling his own supernatural space. The child/baby image is stripped of innocence, made sexually aware and the potential guilt associated with a watcher's gaze on him is assuaged by the child's own 'guilty' voyeuristic focus on the naked miniature adults that dance around him, seemingly at his whim and command.

In the reverse direction, miniature characters easily move from adult novels into children's texts. It was not long, for example, before Part I ('A Voyage to Lilliput') of *Travels into Several Remote Nations of the World by Lemuel Gulliver, first a surgeon, and then a captain of several ships* (Swift 1726) began to appear on its own, particularly in versions produced for children. The 1992 catalogue from the Renier Collection's exhibition *Trash or Treasure* notes that: 'Versions for children of this classic traveller's tale began to appear in the early 19th century' (Chester 1992: 25) and advises that these 'usually consist of either the voyage to Lilliput or Brobdinag, or both' (in the list of related exhibits that follows this comment, seven out of the twelve items relate specifically to Lilliput or a variant name 'Pigmyland'). The Lilliputians have also reappeared with new child protagonists to replace Swift's Gulliver in fictional narratives such as Willis Hall's *Antelope Company* books (and television series) from the 1980s and in T. H. White's (1947) *Mistress Masham's Repose* (see Part II). As with 'Tom Thumb', the name of Lilliput has also been associated consistently with productions for children which are unrelated to any textual version of the story: the Christie's catalogue of *The Marjorie Moon Collection of Early English Children's Books*, for example, contains items such as *The Lilliputian Magazine: or, the young gentleman and lady's golden library* (first published in 1751) and a child's miniature library, *The Cabinet of Lilliput. Stored with instruction and delight* (1802).

Is there more to such global, trans-temporal fascination with the miniature than the portrayal of an intriguing freak or desirable possession and the attendant association of such creations with narratives and artefacts for living children? It seems to me, as I hope to demonstrate, that there must be, that the symbolic resonance of these tiny creatures, as Jung and Bachelard suggest, far exceeds the minute nature of their imaginal appearances and could be regarded as the heart of a culture's collective engagement with 'otherness'.

Speaking of the child motif alone, beyond the polarities of positive and negative, the 'good' and the shadow, of appearances in the image of a female or male bodily form (though these may all feature in the engagement) the idea of the child archetype 'represents a synthesis of the ("divine," i.e., not yet humanized) unconscious and human consciousness' (Jung in Jung and Kerényi 1963: 85) in preparation for the emergence of the self, of which Jung says 'its "absolutely other," is the *sine qua non* of all empirical knowledge and consciousness of subject and object' (1963: 90). In the image of a miniature creature, the already potent symbolic content undergoes condensing and enriching (Bachelard), with the paradoxical presence of powerlessness and power vividly, metaphorically, represented. The significance cannot be overstated, for, as Jung suggests: 'The "child" [speaking of the child motif] is born out of the womb of the unconscious, begotten out of the depths of living Nature herself' (Jung in Jung and Kerényi 1963: 89).

Rooting discussion of this symbol in *Essays on a Science of Mythology*, drawing both on Jung's essay 'The Psychology of the Child Archetype' and Kerényi's 'The Primordial Child in Primordial Times' (see pp. 14, 21), attention is immediately drawn to certain traits that tend to accompany manifestations of the child archetype. Kerényi maintains that the 'child god is usually an abandoned foundling' and faces 'extraordinary dangers' (Kerényi in Jung and Kerényi 1963: 27). He emphasises the child's '*solitariness*' yet the extent to which 'he is . . . *at home* in the primeval world – an equivocal situation, at once that of the orphan child and a cherished son of the gods' (Kerényi in Jung and Kerényi 1963: 28). Jung concurs: 'it is a wonder-child, a divine child, begotten, born, and brought up in quite extraordinary circumstances' (Jung in Jung and Kerényi 1963: 80). In the form of the miniature such traits are emphasised; frequently the tiny child arrives as the result of a wish or prayer, mediated by a witch (as with Thumbelina) or wizard or magician (as with Tom Thumb). Such miraculous conception at once marks them out as 'other' to and distanced from the 'real' world of any culture and from the 'flesh-and-blood' children who inhabit it.

In *The History of Tom Thumbe, the Little, for his small stature surnamed, King Arthvrs Dwarfe: Whose Life and aduentures containe many strange and wonderfull accidents, published for the delight of merry Time-spenders*[9] (1621) (reproduced by Iona and Peter Opie in *The Classic Fairytales*) the magician/wizard character, Merlin, announces:

Ere thrice the Moone her brighnes change,
A shapelesse child by wonder strange,
Shall come abortiue from thy wombe,
No bigger then thy husbands Thumbe:
And as desire hath him begot,
He shall haue life, but substance not;
No blood, nor bones in him shall grow,
Not seene, but when he pleaseth so:
His shapelesse shadow shall be such,
You'l heare him speake, but not him touch:
And till the World to ending come,
There shall be Tales told of Tom Thumbe.
(Opie and Opie 1974: 34)

In Japanese folktale, an elderly couple pray at a shrine before being 'rewarded' with Issun-boshi: 'But small indeed was the child – no larger than a grown man's fingertip' (folkloreandmyth.netfirms.com/japan.html 2006: pages unnumbered). (I should stress here that I am indebted to a colleague, Dr Tamoko Masaki, for confirmation of the robustness of incidents recorded in various sources of the 'Issun-boshi' tale.)

Hans Andersen's heroine, Tömmelise (frequently translated as Thumbelina or Inchelina), arises from within a flower which sprouts from a grain of barley given to a childless woman in response to her plea to an 'old witch' for 'a tiny little child' (Andersen 1994: 29) – linking her with Jung's observation that '[s]ometimes the child appears in the cup of a flower' (*CW* 9i: 270). Jean Ingelow's Mopsa is first to be found in a nest in the hollow of a 'very great thorn tree' (Ingelow 1912: 2).

Miniature literature can be seen, then, to represent a broad spectrum of the genres and mediums that occur in children's literature as a whole, including the appearance of their characters both inside and outside the domain's texts. Beyond this, miniature characters in their earliest fairytale forms demonstrate many of the characteristics Jung and Kerényi associate with instances of the child motif. As the characters begin to appear in composite forms, allied with images of other archetypes and overlaid by 'classic realist' constructions of simulated child psyches, they are ripe for exploration, in search of the effects of this most potent amalgam of symbolic and mimetic content.

Part I

Foreword to Part I

In Chapter 1, I have suggested that miniature characters may enter the children's literature domain in forms that are open to interpretation as 'simple' moment-specific images, metaphorically representing archetypal content from the collective unconscious. In fact such appearances are far from 'simple', but I am using the label here to indicate the lack of overlay of any conscious authorial attempts to create a simulated child persona. In some ways, this also aligns with Marie-Louise von Franz's views,[10] referring to fairytales in general, with regard to the simplicity and purity of such expressions (von Franz 1996: 1).

As part of the fairytale cast of characters, manikins tend to appear and reappear rather than being fixed in any particular single text, and to have arisen in the children's literature domain by virtue of being appropriated by adults who market, publish or buy fiction for children (it does appear as if any 'little' character is regarded as suitable fare for those regarded as 'little' versions of adults). The fictions (frequently multiple) in which they appear are generally retellings of traditional fairytales and myths or invented fairytales.

In this part of the book, I am looking at such 'simple' forms in readiness for an exploration of fantasy texts in which these 'proto-characters', as they may be termed, reappear, embedded within the more elaborately constructed characters that are the cast of fantasy fictions *specifically created* (rather than adapted) for an audience of children. I am focusing on manikins in fairytales from Britain, Japan, Scandinavia and western Europe since these have relevance as antecedents for the characters in the fantasy fictions I shall be engaging with in Part II.

Jung stresses the importance of regarding myth and fairytale as giving metaphorical form to unconscious processes (see, for example, discussion in 'Archetypes of the Collective Unconscious' (*CW* 9i: 6) and in 'The Phenomenology of the Spirit in Fairytales' (*CW* 9i: 400–53)). Drawing on these ideas, von Franz, in works such as *The Interpretation of Fairy Tales* (1970), goes so far as to suggest that fairy tales all metaphorically explore the path of *self-realisation* or *individuation* (see Jung's discussion of these terms in *CW* 7ii: 266–95).[11] The idea of the fairytale as metaphorical expression of such a process is something I will be exploring in relation to the various fairytales that feature in this part of my study. My case studies in Part I will provide me with a base from which to compare and contrast underlying fairytale elements disguised within the twentieth-century literary fantasies for children in Part II.

In drawing together my fairytale case studies, I am aware that it is almost impossible to locate *truly* original and 'pure' forms of any fairytale, given that these are long lost in the ether by virtue of being ephemeral oral tellings. Even in well-regarded collections, such as the Grimms' early nineteenth-century publications, editorial hands, with all that implies by way of chrono-topical and personal influences, may be detected manipulating different editions of the tales. It is a popular misconception, for example, that the Grimms' tales were all 'originally' collected from German peasant women. Jack Zipes records that many of the storytellers used by the Grimms were 'educated young women from the middle-class or aristocracy' (Zipes 1992: xxiv) and identifies particular families who contributed to the work. He also suggests that the brothers incorporated 'stylistic, formal, and substantial thematic changes to appeal to a growing middle-class audience' (Zipes 1992: xxv), going on to note that in later editions of the tales (Zipes offers specific examples of changes made between the 1812 and 1857 editions) the Grimms 'eliminated erotic and sexual elements that might be offensive to middle-class morality, added numerous Christian expressions and references, [and] emphasized specific role models for male and female protagonists according to the dominant patriarchal code of that time' (Zipes 1992: xxviii). Elsewhere Donald Haase (1999) supports this assessment, saying that the tales arose from 'highly educated informants or printed literary texts [and that] Wilhelm Grimm [. . .] freely revised, edited, added to, and basically rewr[ote] many of the classic tales to reflect his own aesthetic and moral values' (Haase 1999: 359–60).

Haase, in particular, uses this revelation as part of a critique of psychoanalytic (and other) readings of fairytales. However, in my view, this is not necessarily a fatal blow to the legitimacy of examining fairytales from a Jungian perspective. It is always possible to look at a variety of versions of fairytales or a myth, surrounding any particular theme or character type, to see what it is that identifies these as related, and what marks them out as different. Even 'simple' characters may draw together within them a jigsaw puzzle image composed of underlying unconscious content and content that is local and personal (to the teller). Choosing to focus on miniature characters makes it easier to compare and contrast tales – what is the same, what is different, how do chrono-topical and personal forces interact to re-'dress' deeper content in the fashions dictated by the moment in which each tale is set down? Jung's oft-quoted words (see below) give both encouragement and warning for anyone engaging with a project of this kind:

> Not for a moment dare we succumb to the illusion that an archetype can be finally explained and disposed of. Even the best attempts at explanation are only more or less successful translations into another metaphorical language. (Indeed, language itself is only an image.) The most we can do is to *dream the myth onwards* and give it a modern dress. And whatever explanation or interpretation does to it, we do to our own souls as well, with corresponding results for our own well-being.
>
> (Jung in Jung and Kerényi 1963: 79, original emphasis)

Chapter 2

Fairytale manikins

Tom Thumb

My first case study draws on early English versions of the 'Tom Thumb' story, predominantly one that Iona and Peter Opie suggest is 'the earliest extant printing of an English fairy tale' (Opie and Opie 1974: 30). According to details provided by the Opies, the 1621 text (currently the only known copy of this is located in Pierpont Morgan Library, New York) is 'a forty-page booklet, printed in London for Thomas Langley' (Opie and Opie 1974: 30) and has the lengthy title *The History of Tom Thumbe, the Little, for his small stature surnamed, King Arthvrs Dwarfe: Whose Life and aduentures containe many strange and wonderfull accidents, published for the delight of merry Time-spenders*. The text is reproduced in the Opies' study of *The Classic Fairy Tales*, with the following details: 'The author of this tale, or the man who gave it shape and set it down seems to have been a Londoner, Richard Johnson (1573–1659?)' (Opie and Opie 1974: 30).

Despite Stith Thompson's (1946) focus on similarities (see Chapter 1) between versions of the 'Tom Thumb' tale, this account, in common with other early English versions, seems to follow a distinctively linear episodic narrative, which is quite unlike continental counterparts. The Opies go so far as to suggest that it is 'a glorious idea rather than a glorious story' (Opie and Opie 1974: 30). Mainland European versions of tales about thumb-sized males, such as Perrault's 'Le petit Poucet' (1697), exhibit a more rounded plot-line, following Propp's functions (see Tatar 1999: 382–7) in terms of the hero leaving home, undergoing trials and tribulations and returning in triumph. Perrault's tale is of the youngest child of seven who saves his larger siblings from death at the hands of an ogre, despite parental abandonment, and is rather more related to the 'Hansel and Gretel' type of tale. Even the Grimms' 'Daumesdick' (1819), perhaps the version which bears the closest similarity to the English 'Tom Thumb' story, in that it contains two sequences in which the protagonist is swallowed by animals, still has a more coherent storyline, complete with happy ending. Thumbling (as Zipes translates the character's name) encourages his parents to accept money offered by strangers for him, eventually making his way back to his relieved mother and father after outwitting his purchasers and a pair of robbers, being swallowed by a cow and a wolf, and outwitting the latter by luring it to his home where his parents can intercede and kill the creature, effecting his release.

The English 'Tom Thumb' character, referred to in Johnson's (1621) title as 'King Arthvrs Dwarfe', meshes with Jung's and Kerényi's ideas concerning appearances of the child motif, in that Tom's conception and birth are miraculous (see Chapter 1) and mediated by a magician figure named Merlin. In the first part of a text that separates into two quite distinct segments the protagonist is presented by the storyteller as vulnerable yet irrepressible, seemingly a conjoint child/hero/trickster figure, emphasising the powerless/powerful paradox inherent in the first of these. This segment is a profane, carnivalesque narrative,[12] in which Tom Thumb's vulnerability (always related to his abnormally small size in relation to the conventionally sized human characters, objects and animals that surround him) is exploited in each of the episodes that occur once he has been born. Tom's responses to each of these challenges to his safety are in the 'trickster/braggart' spectrum: as a 'prankster' and 'pickpocket' cheating his play-fellows at games; as a 'rumpus-rouser' when engulfed in a pudding, a cow's and later a giant's stomach; as a quick-thinking nimble 'out-witter' who alternately hides and then tries to talk his way out of trouble. Whenever engulfed by larger objects or characters that accidentally or deliberately consume him, he stamps his identity and presence on the situation, in order to obtain release.

Tom can be read in Jungian terms as a metaphorical image of archetypal content, arising in the form of the child-archetype. His visible vulnerability, due to his diminutive size, ensures that the 'child' is conjoined with the image of a trickster, since trickstersh activity is the only response to danger that is available, within the narrative, to enable the tiny creature to survive at this stage of the tale. Prior to the intervention of supernatural power (which occurs in the second segment of this telling of the tale), such a response is all that can assist in redressing the balance between minute child and the gigantic world that so carelessly consumes him. Johnson speaks of the character having 'a desperate little spirit, like to his small bignesse' (Opie and Opie 1974: 35), writing some 320 years before Jung's comment that the 'motif of "smaller than small yet bigger than big" complements the impotence of the child by means of its equally miraculous deeds' (Jung in Jung and Kerényi 1963: 83–4).

Following von Franz's lead in seeing fairytales as metaphorical explorations of the path of self-realisation (see Foreword to Part I), Tom Thumb could also conceivably be regarded as a conjoint ego, hero and trickster image within a text that metaphorically represents the journey of such a figure into the unconscious. Looking from a psychoanalytical perspective at the character and the ways in which he is depicted continually resisting attempts to swallow him up one can see an ego figure initially resisting immersion in the unconscious, with particular emphasis on maternal aspects of the unconscious. Remembering that Audhumla the cow, created from melt-ice at the beginning of time, is instrumental in forming the first man in Norse mythology, it is likely to be significant that Tom is taken into the cow's body, but resists, vigorously, being incorporated into this re-visioning of archetypal primeval maternal. Johnson as storyteller describes, vividly, the manikin being swallowed up in a single mouthful, resisting by shouting and dancing vigorously in the cow's belly (to that creature's considerable discomfort), and only eventually obtaining release when a laxative drink is given to the cow. Tom reappears in the outer world in a cow turd, expelled, forcibly, from a second maternal body (see Opie and Opie 1974: 38).

In story terms, the character's earliest encounter with the maternal is his birth mother, whom he experiences as something of a negative figure. She is not the one who is portrayed as longing for a child on her own account, she is merely obedient to her husband's wishes to procure one by magical means. Tom is conceived only when his birth mother is persuaded by her husband to visit Merlin's cave and beg the magician to 'discouer the cause of thy barrenesse, and bee a meanes to procreate vs children: Away, and of him procure this good blessing, be hee no bigger then my very Thumbe' (Opie and Opie 1974: 33). Later, when she fears that her tiny son is drowned in her pudding mix, the storyteller complains that she is quick to abandon the child and make the best of things 'she ouerpassed her losse in a short time (I might say a minutes space) especially considering him to be a child (for his littlenesse,) more disgraceful, then comfortable' (Opie and Opie 1974: 36). Tom is not so lightly cast away. Having created a rumpus in the kettle, while being cooked, and frightening his mother into giving the pudding that contains him to a tinker begging at the door (fearing it to be possessed of a demonic spirit), Tom effects his release in similar manner. He creates a rumpus from inside the pudding, which frightens the tinker so much that he 'fart[s] for very feare' (Opie and Opie 1974: 36). Then Tom's apparently disembodied voice, exclaiming at the man's noisy farting, increases the tinker's terror so much that he drops his bag, complete with pudding and tools, and runs away, leaving Tom at liberty to eat his way out of his temporary (maternally created) prison. Again the incarceration in the pudding seems to imply an attempted devouring of the character, with the pudding feasibly seen (having been prepared and cooked by Tom's mother) as if it is part of the maternal sphere – quick to engulf the tiny child.

When Tom is eventually carried completely away from home by a bird, the teller of the tale also casts that creature as female. The bird is a raven, associated with evil by some sources (see Jung's notes to 'The Phenomenology of the Spirit in Fairytales' in *CW* 9i: 428n), but it is her sex that is probably more significant here. The manikin is mistaken for a grain of wheat, taken up in a raven's beak, and swiftly transported away from his home over a vast forest. He continually frightens the raven with his desperate cries, so that she is afraid to swallow the tiny creature and equally afraid of dropping him.

The child motif is also represented in the ego's shadow form in this version of the 'Tom Thumb' tale, this time hyperbolically, in the shape of the first giant that Tom Thumb outwits. Discovered by Tom when the manikin is dropped by his female raven abductor into the creature's castle, the shadow archetype appears as a demonic form, characterised by insatiable and uncontrollable appetites, 'sitting by his fire, boyling, broiling and roasting the ioynts & quarters of men, deuouring them all one after another, legs, armes & heads bit by bit till they were all eaten vp at last' (Opie and Opie 1974: 39). At this stage in the fairytale Tom Thumb has no magical gifts to protect him, so his response to danger is to outwit the giant who, childlike, despite Tom's usefulness (the giant having been persuaded to employ the manikin), cannot resist attempting to catch and eat the tiny creature. From a Jungian perspective, this appears as a story moment which could be read as a metaphorical envisioning of ego being incorporated, voluntarily, into 'his' shadow counterpart (as represented by the character jumping down the giant's throat) yet resisting annihilation in the encounter – in story terms by vigorous movement, which eventually causes the giant to vomit up the tiny hero (Opie and Opie 1974: 40).

At this stage, the manikin is swallowed for the last time, and this signals a move into the second phase of the story. Having been ejected with the Giant's vomit, Tom Thumb falls into the sea, where a fish swallows him alive. The fish swims, with Tom inside (this time acquiescent and peacefully enveloped), across the sea, being eventually caught and served at King Arthur's table. When the fish is cut open, Tom Thumb is revealed and emerges safe and sound – interestingly resonant with the idea of the birth of the first human beings from fish, a doctrine emanating from the Greek philosopher Anaximander (see Kerényi in Jung and Kerényi 1963: 46; von Franz 1996: 154).

There may well be archetypal significance in the mode of the manikin's transition, for the fish is frequently regarded as a symbolic creature in ritual, myth and fairytale. In *The Golden Bough* (1922) Sir James Frazer points to instances of the fish as a respected, even sacred being (Frazer 1957: 473, 527) and Kerényi and von Franz both remind readers of Christian symbolic usage of the fish, in association with the Christ figure (Kerényi in Jung and Kerényi 1963: 46; von Franz 1970: 154). In mythological terms, both Jung and Kerényi link the image of a fish with the idea of the sea as primordial uterus (Jung in Jung and Kerényi 1963: 150–1; Kerényi in Jung and Kerényi 1963: 46–5).

Interestingly, in Frazer's chapter on 'The External Soul in Folk-Tales' there is also an account of a Malayan poem in which the female protagonist's soul is said to be placed for safe-keeping inside a golden fish (Frazer 1957: 676–7). The girl in the poem is of mysterious origins that assert the presence of an image of the child motif, and thus link 'her' tale with that of Tom Thumb. A foundling, she is discovered, so the poem recounts, on a river bank by a childless couple. In the 'Tom Thumb' tale, Tom is, effectively, reborn from the fish, perhaps a metaphorical enactment of the ego, having encountered the shadow, entering the depths of the unconscious to reach and engage with other archetypal figures in the symbolic form of the courtiers, the Queen and the ruling King at King Arthur's Court.

It is here in King Arthur's Court that Tom as ego-hero encounters what may be interpreted as a plethora of images of 'his' anima, altogether more erotic in tone than earlier maternal images. Here, following 'his rebirth', he is introduced to the female domain once more:

> The ladies and Gentlewomen could seldome bee without him; for his company was so pleasing, that many times they gaue him leaue to sleepe vpon their knees, and now and then in their pockets, with many such like priuate places, [. . .] and to runne at tilt against their bosomes with a bul-rush.
>
> (Opie and Opie 1974: 41)

This particular telling of the tale does not, however, punish the sexually awakened child/trickster/hero unlike some other versions, such as the ballad which ends:

> Into a spider's web he fell,
> And could not hence get free.
> The spider watching for his prey
> Took Tom to be a fly,
> And seized him without delay,
> Regarding not his cry.
> The blood out of his body drains,
> He yielded up his breath;
> Thus he was freed from all his pains,
> By his unlook'd for death
> (Wright, 1700[?], reproduced by
> Ashton 1969: 220–1)

Here death is visited on the protagonist by the storyteller, who 'punishes' the character for overstepping the perceived bounds of the divine-child–trickster alliance by adding 'sexual' tricks to his 'prankster' repertoire and by attempting dalliance with the Queen (doubly tabooed as she is both wife and royal – perhaps introducing a link with the Guinevere of Arthurian legend): 'For his desires were lustful grown/ Against her Majesty,/ Finding of her one day alone,/ Which proved his tragedy' (Wright, 1700[?], reproduced by Ashton 1969: 219).

A more benign face of the anima is introduced earlier into Johnson's telling of the tale, however, for the 'Queen of Fayres' (Opie and Opie 1974: 34) (later spelled as 'Queen of Fayries': Opie and Opie 1974: 35), is the 'midnights Midwife' (Opie and Opie 1974: 34) who delivers the miniature child and provides him with his first items of clothing. She provides another hinge between the segments of the story, bringing enchanted gifts to aid the protagonist in his new life at King Arthur's court. The Fairy Queen magically provides her godson with a quaternity of enchanted objects, including a 'Ring likewise inchanted', which could be interpreted as symbolising the self (see Jung's discussion of such symbolic representations: *CW* 6: 790). Drawing in the masculine sphere, the Fairy Queen's ring is matched by a golden one which King Arthur presents to Tom for his prowess at dancing the galliard.

From this story moment onwards, there is a reduction in the character's dependence on his trickster aspect and an absence of the powerlessness associated with the child archetype. The trickster is transcended, as the ego-hero dons the magical gifts and assimilates their powers: the 'smaller than small' becomes 'bigger than big' (see p. 35). Significantly it is connectedness with the Fairy Queen, the beneficent aspect of the feminine,[13] coming to him in his sleep, yet apprehended through his dreams, that empowers Tom and leads him into what might be interpreted as individuation and a new authority that his miniature size can no longer diminish:

> [the Queene of Fayries] found her little God-sonne asleepe (in the Kings Garden) vpon the toppe of a Red Rose new blowne. And [. . .] she stood inuisibly before him, stroaking downe the sweaty droppes with her vnfelt hand from his little forehead, which cast him into a most sweete and pleasurable dreame, and withal bestowed foure of the most rarest guifts of the world vpon him, which she left there lying by against his awaking. First, an inchanted Hat, the which by wearing hee should know, what was done in all parts of the world. A Ring likewise inchanted, that hauing it vpon his finger, hee might goe if hee pleased into any place vnseene, and walke inuisible. Thirdly, a Girdle, that by wearing it, should change him into what shape soeuer he desired. And lastly, a payre of shooes, (that being on his feete) would in a moment carry him to any part of the earth, and to be any time where hee pleased. Thus with a feruency of loue blessed shee him, and departed.
>
> (Opie and Opie 1974: 43)

As the above passage demonstrates, the imagery in Johnson's account of this dream encounter is redolent with a sense of a male encounter with anima. Yet, the encounter is, in story terms, that which occurs between Tom and his fairy godmother. The magical queen and the earthly queen are set in contrast and it is the first of these and not the latter who symbolically draws the 'child' into a magical (by means of the gifts) and newly powerful incarnation.

Later, Tom, aided by his supernatural gifts, encounters an even more fearsome giant – Garagantua. At this stage in the tale (see the relevant passage quoted by Opie and Opie 1974: 45–6), under the influence of the gifts that have transformed him, Tom has moved from the child's spectrum of boisterous activity to the adult spectrum where he exhibits a tone of 'moral' superiority. As image of ego drawn into close association with governing archetype there is an intimation that 'he' has adult knowledge which is guarded from the childish opponents the character encounters. Partnered by the depiction of a beneficent anima figure, the former trickster is shown adopting a heroic response as his encounter with the Garagantua (whose size again may hyperbolically represent uncontrolled childish appetites) demonstrates. Here an intriguing boasting match is a carnivalesque battle in which both participants claim advantage for themselves from 'human' activities exaggerated at opposite ends of the spectrum by the abnormal size of their perpetrators. Significantly, an absence of uncontrolled bodily desires and appetites characterises the renewed manikin in contrast to the greedy and murderous form of the shadow child's boasts.

Offering a personal interpretation, the English 'Tom Thumb' tale, with its episodic roots (Opie and Opie (1974: 31) go so far as to suggest that it 'almost seems to be the prototype fairytale'), suggests a worrying engagement with what Jung refers to as the 'time-spirit' (see p. 15) of its age's reimagining of archetypal characters. With its violent rejection of the bodily maternal sphere and seemingly tabooed sexual engagement it offers the heroic role model of a troubled mind/body/spirit relationship. The child/hero/ego figure has no need of 'foode or sustenance' (Opie and Opie 1974: 35), is punished for or rises above sexual activity, and moves from the trickster spectrum into engagement with the spiritual-maternal anima, so that masculine and feminine are conjoined in the fairy godmother's touch and the dual rings from King Arthur and the Fairy Queen; all surmounted by the quaternity of enchanted gifts. The birth mother, earthly queen and sexualised female courtiers are left behind; the chthonic is condemned and the maternal and Fairy Queen (perhaps the 'madonna' of the madonna/whore dichotomy) is the (significantly portrayed as invisible) feminine that assists in bringing wholeness to the text as psychodynamic process.

Issun-boshi

The eponymous protagonist of the Japanese tale, 'Issun-boshi' (Little Inchkin) also aligns with Jungian ideas concerning the child archetype, but here the figure is conjoint with the hero aspect; the trickster spectrum of activity is largely absent (although there is one dissenting account in this respect – see below and p. 43). Unlike his episodic English counterpart, Issun-boshi, in similar fashion to the German 'Daumesdick' and the French 'Le petit Poucet', follows a rounded narrative, in which the overt morality discernible in the story praises hard work and courage, ending, significantly, with achievement by the manikin of a full man's height and marriage with the Princess.

It is more difficult to locate the actual text or any early English translations of publications of the story of Issun-boshi, primarily due to language difficulties. However, commentary on the bare bones of the narrative suggests that the tale, through numerous versions, has broadly similar beginnings and endings and that story events are largely the same. Virginia Skord (1991) mentions that the storyline surfaced in medieval Japanese literature and comments: 'The tiny hero with hidden dynamic power may be traced to legendary figures associated with the thundergod, and it is no wonder that, in almost all stories in which he appears, ultimately he is revealed to be a god' (Skord 1991: 115). Following on from this suggestion of the 'divine' origins of the miniature child, Rambelli and Teeuwen (2002) speak of 'the folktale motif of a child possessing great strength, as in the story of Issun-boshi (Little one-inch), who despite his size, subjugates two demons' (citing Hisamoto Shimazu's account of 1929). The character, in the form of a 'little child', carries a 'mallet [. . .] with him, which will make him grow to normal size upon striking his body' (Rambelli and Teeuwen 2002: 60).

Noriko Reider (2003) gives further details of the story, citing Ichiko's account of 1958 as the source. Unusually, in this particular text, the character does behave in trickster fashion at one point in the story and I shall return to this later. All the versions of the folktale I have encountered begin with the miraculous conception:

> In the story, a boy is born to an elderly couple who are well beyond the years of conception and childbirth. For years, the couple had been praying to a deity so that they might conceive. The child the woman gives birth to, however, a boy, never grows big, and remains as small as one inch.
>
> (Reider 2003: 133)

Similarly, a variety of internet sources confirm this part of the storyline:

> Long, long ago there lived a sweet old couple. Having no children but desiring one very much, they went to the shrine and prayed, 'Please, please let us have a child, no matter how small.' Eventually, a son was born to them. But small indeed was the child – no larger than a grown man's fingertip.
>
> The couple raised the child tenderly, and though he became a bright and well-respected young man, he grew not at all. As a result, he became known as Issun-boshi (issun is a unit measuring about 3 centimeters).
>
> (http://folkloreandmyth.netfirms.com/japan.html 2006)

> Issun Boshi was a tiny hero. [H]is parents were childless for many years and they prayed for a child even if [it] was only the size of the end of a finger. Oddly enough they got what they asked for in a rather literal sense.
>
> (http://quasisemi.com/myth/i.htm 2006)

> Once long ago in Japan there lived a couple who had no children. They prayed to the gods for a child, even one as small as a finger, and finally their prayers were answered. The child born to them was so small that they named him Issun Boshi, 'Little One Inch'.
>
> (http://dimdima.com/khazana/stories/show_globalstories.asp?q_id=153&q_title=Little+One+Inch&q_country=Japan 2006)

In all the above versions the character is portrayed as a resourceful young man, who, in due course, sets out in search of fame and fortune. Unlike the English 'Tom Thumb' the manikin leaves home voluntarily and none of the storytellers suggests that the child is exposed to danger by his mother. (I am grateful to Dr Tamoko Masaki, a colleague at Roehampton University at the time I began my research into miniature literature, for confirming that the events set down in English translations of this Japanese folktale are broadly the same as those recorded in versions of the tale in the original Japanese.) In a colourful version specifically designed and marketed for children, Fiona French (1994) brings her own interpretive skills to embellishing the tale by emphasising the character's dauntlessness, despite his tiny stature:

> Making a sharp sword out of a needle and millet straw, and a strong suit of armour out of beetles' wings, Inchkin practised fighting crickets and bumblebees, and even a big mouse. He became a skilled swordsman.
>
> (French 1994: picturebook with no page numbering)

In the central part of the story the miniature man finds employment at the house of a wealthy nobleman – here the Reider (2003) version records a trickster response: 'He finds a job as a servant of an aristocratic family and falls madly in love with the couple's beautiful daughter. Tricked by Little One-Inch, the daughter is banished and comes under his care' (Reider 2003: 133). Other tales simply say that he finds favour in the household, becoming the daughter's attendant.

The tales come together again, however, when Issun-boshi and the daughter are attacked by oni (evil spirits). The swallowing of the character by one of the ogres is similar to the episode in the 'Tom Thumb' story when the giant attempts to eat the protagonist, but in this instance the tiny character is armed with a sword and able to defend himself.

One of the oni eats Little One-Inch in one gulp but the boy fights against the oni, plunging his little sword into the being from inside its body. Defeated, the oni coughs up Little One-Inch and the band of demons scamper away, leaving behind a magical wish-granting mallet (Reider 2003: 133).

The wish-granting mallet – in some versions wielded by the Lord's daughter (or, as she is frequently named, princess) – allows Little One-Inch to be transformed to 'normal human' size and gain riches through its supernatural power. Needless to say he marries the princess. The most recent of the retellings used here omits the swallowing incident and the wish-giving mallet – nevertheless, the protagonist still vanquishes the demons, is granted full size, and marries.

> Suddenly two fiery demons who had strayed down from the mountains blocked their way.

> The princess went pale, but Inchkin gripped his tiny sword, ready to defend her with his life.
>
> 'Come any closer and I will kill you!' he cried.
>
> The two demons were astonished.
>
> One of them loomed over him. 'You are very frightening,' he sneered. 'Why, I could eat you in one mouthful!'
>
> Inchkin lunged at him with his sharp sword.
>
> 'Aieee!' cried the demon.
>
> Before the other demon knew what was going on, Inchkin leapt between them.
>
> Shouting a fierce battle-cry, he swung his sword in the air and stabbed him hard in the nose.
>
> The demon howled with pain and both the evil spirits fled away.
>
> At that moment the temple bells began to ring and, as each pure note rang out across the mountains, Inchkin felt himself grow taller and taller. The Lord Buddha was rewarding him for his bravery by granting his dearest wish.
>
> (French 1994: picture book with no page numbering)

The spectacular transformation of the tiny character is particularly potent as a metaphorical vehicle.[14] The idea of a miniature-being transformed, in a moment, from a state of minute 'otherness' into a 'normal-sized' adult person is a powerful image, capable of leaving a strong visual imprint on the minds of readers. In a psychoanalytic interpretation of Issun-boshi as metaphorical ego-hero and child-archetype in the text, the 'child' is shown successfully separating from the benign mother and father figure and finding and joining his anima; ultimately he is depicted as able both to incorporate with the hyperbolic-shadow child (in the form of the oni) and to break free through his own efforts. Both the supernatural mallet (hammer in some versions) and the 'Lord Buddha' of French's version can readily be interpreted as images of the self, so that, with the appearance of the governing archetype, Issun-boshi is able to grow in what can be interpreted as a metaphorical representation of individuating. The metaphorical child archetype splits away and the ego-hero can be seen as representing an archetypal pattern of inner maturation, yet also having an outer resonance in terms of an adult-envisaged idea of 'child' linking successfully with the erotic 'other' and growing into his stable 'adult' self through hard work, dedication and bravery in a society in which such qualities are valued. Significantly, in symbolic terms, the tale suggests that for the male subject a positive encounter with anima gives motive to engaging with the shadow (here combatively in physical symbolism – compare this with the verbal confrontation between Tom Thumb and Garagantua) and facilitates the emergence of the self.

Contrasting these early tales of miniature-male characters it can be seen that, at the deepest levels, they do share in the creation of images which express archetypal propensities and that these are overlaid with ideas of female 'otherness' and characteristics conventionally labelled as 'feminine' and 'masculine' (see note 13). Similarly, they suggest a deeply felt need for there to be some form of engagement with 'otherness', as here, between male character and 'feminine' sphere. There is also a vivid visual enactment of conflict with the shadow, in the form of the hyperbolic child with 'his' uncontrollable appetites. Both characters depict an active and violent struggle to survive incorporation into the shadow – whether this is associated with the child-archetype (both) or with negatively regarded human and animal forms of the mother-archetype (Tom Thumb).

Where the stories move apart, the early English tale shows a level of conflict with the 'feminine' sphere represented in the negative maternal images which seems to be absent in the Japanese version. However, it should be said that this may be due to the Japanese tale being a more 'finished' story – perhaps further from its roots, with significant detail repressed. In the English version, the writer (or possibly writers/storytellers, since details are likely to have arisen in earlier 'tellings' and 'retellings') imagines a 'little man' as conjoined child/ego/trickster figure thrown breathlessly into a maelstrom of activity in which connectedness with a spiritual 'feminine' is the only pathway to an individuation in which the ego can survive. In this, the 'rawest' state of the fairytale, there seems to be an expression of 'longing' for some form of numinous 'madonna'-like female figure and a corresponding fear of engulfment in the matriarchal body. In Part II I shall be looking at more complex character formations and questioning whether this hidden content underlies twentieth-century literary engagement with the miniature.

Chapter 3

Nineteenth-century female miniatures

Thumbelina

By contrast with the early male 'Tom Thumb' and 'Issun-boshi' miniature characters, in this chapter I am examining female protagonists from two nineteenth-century literary fairytales, one created by Hans Christian Andersen in Denmark (1836) and one by Jean Ingelow in England (1869). Although these are more discernibly the work of individual writers, the miniature protagonists are still very one-dimensional 'simple' character formations, with much that relates them to fairytale, rather than the kind of characterisation currently associated with more 'novel-like' stories for children. The first of these characters is Andersen's Tömmelise – a name popularly translated into English as Thumbelina or Inchelina[15] – eponymous heroine of a text Andersen terms an 'original fairy tale' (Andersen 1994: 1072), rather than the retelling of a traditional story.

Speaking of his work on 'wholly original' literary fairy tales, Andersen comments: 'They lay in my mind like seeds and only needed a gentle touch – the kiss of a sunbeam or drop of malice – to flower' (Andersen 1994: 1074). The metaphor is an apt one in reference to Tömmelise, since Andersen's tiny protagonist arises from a flower, a tulip, which in turn has sprouted from a grain of barley – sold by an old witch for the sum of twelve pennies ('tolv Skilling').[16] Such extraordinary genesis calls at once to mind the miraculous origins attributed to the child archetype and to Jung's comments, that '[s]ometimes the child appears in the cup of a flower' (Jung in Jung and Kerényi 1963: 78). At this stage in his discussion Jung has moved on from reference to an 'imaginary' child he links specifically with women with 'mental disorders' (Jung in Jung and Kerényi 1963: 78) to a linkage with individuation; however, it is interesting that the child in Andersen's tale arises from an apparently lone and barren woman's wish for a child.

So Andersen's tale of 'Tömmelise' arises from a 'seed' in his mind, a mind that may be seen as inescapably rooted in his own lived experiences, both general and personal, yet still a mind with the propensity to reimagine archetypal content from the collective unconscious. This is not a traditional tale in the accepted sense, despite the style and nomination of fairytale. Unlike the many and various episodic appearances of Tom Thumb, Tömmelise is rooted very firmly in the individual mind of a storyteller, one who wishes to be a visible part of his imagined narrative:

> I wanted the style to be such that the reader felt the presence of the storyteller; therefore the spoken language had to be used. I wrote the stories for children, but older people ought to find them worth listening to.
>
> (Andersen 1994: 1071)

Yet the particular way in which Andersen gives image to archetypal elements in his tale, while having much to say to his own chronotopical and personal context, irrevocably joins a domain of images which, in true inter-narrative fashion, move ever onwards into our own times and beyond. To return to Jung's words (quoted on p. 31): 'The most we can do is to *dream the myth onwards* and give it a modern dress' (Jung in Jung and Kerényi 1963: 79, original emphasis). In his tale, Andersen indeed 'dream[ed]' both 'myth' and child archetype onwards in a way that relates his miniature character to others of both past and future.

This is perhaps a good moment to recall the elements of the story of Tömmelise (here translated as Inchelina):

- Kidnapped by a Toad as a wife for her son, Inchelina faces a life 'down in the mud' (Andersen 1994: 30).
- Seized in the 'claws' of a maybug who desires her loveliness, Inchelina is carried away, only to be abandoned 'all alone in the forest' (Andersen 1994: 32) as the taunts and jibes of the female maybugs convince her captor (and Inchelina herself) that the miniature girl is ugly.
- In the winter forest Inchelina faces death by freezing and starvation.
- Even Inchelina's rescuer, a field mouse, procures her for marriage

with a mole deep under the ground in permanent darkness and, when the girl cries out against such a fate, threatens Inchelina with the words 'Don't be stubborn or I will bite you with my white teeth' (Andersen 1994: 35).

- A creature who revels in nature and in daylight, Inchelina is portrayed as despairing of the life she will live underground and lamenting: '"Farewell . . . Farewell, you beautiful sun!" Inchelina lifted her hands up toward the sky . . . She saw a little red flower. Embracing it, she said: "Farewell! And give my love to the Swallow if you ever see him"' (Andersen 1994: 36).
- But in the style of a fairytale romance written for children, Inchelina the tiny maiden is rescued by the knight-like Swallow, whom she herself had earlier compassionately saved from death, achieving a fairytale escape, a flight from darkness to an ethereal (quasi-spiritual) marriage with a king 'white and almost transparent, as if he were made of glass' (Andersen 1994: 37).

Before delving into the possible symbolic significance of the figures involved in these events, it is helpful to investigate the tale's underlying mythic ancestry. In it one may clearly discern a link with the myth of Persephone's rape and abduction by Aïdoneus (Hades), god of the underworld,[17] also known as Pluto (the brother of her brother/sister father and mother). The abduction, so the tale goes, is carried out with the connivance of Persephone's father, Zeus, and of Gaia, the mother-earth figure of Greek mythology, who (as Kerényi (1931) advises in *The Gods of the Greeks*) 'to please the god of the Underworld . . . caused [a narcissus] to spring up, a radiant wonder, as a wile to seduce the maiden with the rosebud countenance' (Kerényi 1931: 232). As daughter of Demeter, the corn goddess, Persephone has been compared (and Kerényi comments on this in depth in 'Kore', the third section of *Essays on a Science of Mythology: The Myths of the Divine Child and the Divine Maiden* by Jung and Kerényi) with the seed of the corn, fertilized and buried under the earth for half the year (or in some versions one-third), then released from her fate in the Spring to live life above ground in the fresh air and sunshine.

In the Greek myth, Demeter, the corn goddess, gives birth to a beautiful daughter, Persephone, loses her beneath the earth, yet sees her 'reborn' from the dark earth's womb as the season for seeds to grow and flower begins. In Andersen's tale, a grain of barley is planted, grows and flowers to reveal Tömmelise. In the myth,

Persephone undergoes a marriage in hell. In Andersen's fairytale, Tömmelise, saved from a series of potentially 'hellish' marriages, achieves a union which seems, symbolically, made in heaven, with a 'tiny little king', the king of a host of 'tiny angel[s]' (Andersen 1994: 37).

Andersen's ending can readily be interpreted (perhaps by the 'older people' who Andersen suggests 'ought to find [the stories] worth listening to' (Andersen 1994: 1071) as suggesting that Tömmelise's escape involves a movement from earth to heaven – effectively death – and, instead of rebirth, a heavenly afterlife (with the swallow cast, as birds frequently are, as conveyer of souls to the next life). Yet even here, where the stories diverge, there is still an explicit association in Andersen's tale with ideas of the Greek Gods and Goddesses, since the swallow flies south to where there are 'the ruins of an ancient temple; ivy wound . . . around the white pillars' (Andersen 1994: 36).

So how has Andersen 'dream[ed]' the Persephone myth onward? At first sight it would appear that a reading of Andersen's tale should place Tömmelise at the conscious forefront of its psychodynamic process, a metaphorical representation of ego in the text, but, as Andersen has deliberately interposed the figure of the storyteller between readers and his protagonist, a far more fruitful reading arises from seeing the storyteller as persona to Andersen as ego, with all other characters within the tale as figures in the unconscious of the narrative as metaphorical psychodynamic process. In looking at a reading which explores the ideas of the 'otherness' labelled as 'feminine' that exist within Andersen's text, then Tömmelise, as maiden, is clearly cast in the role of anima. But Jung maintains that a man's 'soul-image' is first borne by the mother, only later transferring to and settling upon what might be termed a 'soul-mate' (to use popular parlance and not Jung's words). This leads Jung to highlight the significance for men of achieving an appropriate and non-traumatic separation from the mother – something he regards as achieved in many earlier societies by means of ritual (*CW* 7: 314).

In a quaternity within the Demeter-Persephone myth the mother-daughter images appear in unity and bonded by love. The male father-uncle and ravisher-bridegroom-uncle dyad are shadow figures, disposing and taking by force. Demeter's grief at separation from her daughter ultimately results in Persephone being restored to her for part of the year: as a maternal archetype, the image of Demeter is that of the 'good' and 'loving' mother, though resisting separation from her offspring. Yet in Andersen's tale, it is the female figures that dispose and force, they are the ones who are almost uniformly given imaginal 'shadow' form.

The old witch sells the maiden-seed to a woman who desires to possess her. The purchaser-mother promises love, yet the story does not recount any effort made by her to search for the tiny child who has been abducted. The character is completely unlike Demeter, who Kerényi, drawing on the Homeric hymn, says 'tore the head-dress from her immortal hair, cast her dark raiment from off her shoulders, and flew like a bird over land and water in search of her child' (Kerényi 1931: 233). The toad mother takes on the role of the abductor in her intention to force the maiden to live in the mud – with her son almost sidelined as would-be ravisher. It is the maybug females that taunt and denigrate the maiden, causing her abandonment in the forest. The field mouse, though saving Inchelina from the winter elements, demands payment in stories and, seeing her as commodity, ultimately threatens her and procures her for would-be-husband mole, introducing her innocent charge to prostitution by marriage for material gain and a life of darkness underground.

It is a shadow matriarchy that is depicted. A 'good' mother image may be read, just possibly, into Andersen's depictions of nature – a particularly 'non-earthy', possibly 'spirit-nature' filled with flowers, sunshine, butterflies and birds. However, significantly (and perversely) everything from ground-level down (where the roots of all this beauty may be found) is associated with mud, with darkness, with blindness to beauty and it is *this* earthiness, murkiness and gloom that Andersen's tale most closely associates with female images of the mother archetype. They form an uncompassionate shadow matriarchy bound to the market place. Many of the male figures may be shadow figures too, not averse to possessing the tiny girl, but they are always portrayed as operating under the encouragement of shadow-mothers and jealous female rivals.

Perhaps the most interesting aspect of the Tömmelise story, when reading the protagonist as metaphorical anima, is size-related. Unlike Persephone, who is presented as a full-sized adolescent maiden at the time of her abduction, Tömmelise is simultaneously child and maiden: 'a tiny little girl . . . so beautiful and so delicate, and exactly one inch long' (Andersen 1994: 5) and, as such, a very potent symbol of certain constructions of femininity and miniaturised vulnerability. That anima, the potentially erotic other, should be associated with a delicate miniaturised girl-child may be read as having considerable significance, particularly in view of what Cox (1996), drawing on Kincaid and others, terms a nineteenth-century phenomenon 'The Cult of the Little Girl':

> 'Innocence', remarks Kincaid, 'is not . . . detected but granted, not nurtured but enforced; it comes at the child as a denial of a whole host of capacities, an emptying out' (Kincaid 1992: 73). And having been, as Kincaid puts it, 'emptied out', the child can be filled with whatever qualities adults choose to favour. Into the little girl were poured qualities of innocence which, though they could be shared by boys to some degree, acquired a special potency in the little girl through the power of her incipient sexuality. In what is frequently termed 'the cult of the little girl', these qualities were reverenced and expressed in terms which to the late twentieth-century mind are often disturbing. [As one might expect, Cox goes on to enter into a detailed discussion of the well-known instances of Kilvert, Ruskin and Dodgson (Carroll), which need not be rehearsed again here.]
>
> (Cox 1996: 153–4)

My point, though, is that Tömmelise may be read as *the* ultimate fantasy expression of erotic 'other' encapsulated in innocent form. She is portrayed as sexually desirable and desired, sexually vulnerable to the most hideous ravishment, yet remains untouched, preserved for a 'marriage made in heaven'. Whether this is all Andersen's personal projection, or one that arises in his chrono-topical moment (as Cox's and Kincaid's words suggest), or mix of these, will always be impossible to do more than speculate upon, although Andersen's possibly ambivalent sexuality is something that was discussed at the conference, *Hans Christian Andersen (1805–2005): A Celebration and Reappraisal*, which was held in August 2005 at the British Library Conference Centre.[18] What *is* certain is that in Andersen's 'dress', Tömmelise, unlike the maiden arising as a possible metaphorical expression of collective archetypal content in earlier myth, is not dragged into an underworld of sexual passion. For Andersen's intra-textual imagining of anima, marriage is made safe in a heavenly setting, in which her 'transparent' (Andersen 1994: 37), angelic and similarly tiny bridegroom offers no hint of bodily grossness to penetrate and destroy her quasi *spiritual* fragility.

Returning to the idea of the fairytale as a metaphorical expression of a movement toward realisation of the 'self' (see von Franz 1996: 2), then Tömmelise's King and bridegroom could well symbolise the 'self' of Andersen's text. This ultimately suggests a reading (and I stress this is merely my own) in which a male figure rendered tiny and vulnerable, thus an expression of the divine child, purged of grossness until he is 'transparent', is the link between what may be termed 'innocent' anima and the masculine ego of the storyteller in an inner 'heaven' – free from dark matriarchal interference and the ego's shadow manifestations in despised (within the text) theriomorphic toad-son, many-clawed maybug and blind mole. Is this a fairytale solution? Is sublimation of masculine sexuality and the absence of matriarchal control of the idealised feminine the desired end of 'self' realisation? If so, it would appear that the combined demonisation and idealisation of women in the madonna/whore dichotomy is as potentially damaging to male subjects as to female subjects. These are important questions to raise and ponder.

Beyond the immediate chrono-topical location of this representation of anima, and moving into the twentieth and twenty-first centuries, I want to suggest that the image of Tömmelise is a potent and enduring one, and long survives the death of its creator. From now on I shall refer to the character by the name most frequently used in today's publications that aim to tell 'her' story – Thumbelina.

A multiplicity of book 'tellings' and 'retellings' surround Andersen's protagonist and, inevitably, there are film and video versions as well – all of which offer their own interpretations of the character. Significantly, in the latter, Thumbelina is wrested from Andersen and claimed as the property of other males, as in the Warner Brothers' video, which is actually entitled *Don Bluth's Thumbelina*. A lot can be said about such interpretations, but this would provide more than enough matter for another chapter. So I will just briefly visit a more surprising manifestation of her image from well beyond the boundaries of western male-dominated media productions. A Chinese writer, Zhang Kangkang, uses the image in her novella *Northern Lights* (1980) as metaphor for the feelings of a female character, Lu Qinqin, who finds herself moving inexorably into a marriage she does not desire but cannot frame 'sensible' reasons for refusing: 'Even if she were in the little dark alley where Thumbelina lived, a pretty swallow might still hurry in the day before her wedding and carry her away to the sunny South' (translated in Bryant 1989: 116). Later, Lu Qinqin catches sight of a little girl ice-skating and associates her, through the colour of her ski cap, with a vivid image of her childhood self (to the extent that she 'feels' as if it is herself she is seeing). She is depicted lamenting the irretrievable loss of her early self (as she imagines herself to have once been) and compares this with Thumbelina's rescue from an earthly marriage:

> Childhood, youth, dreams of spring, they are all going to disappear for good. I really feel like kissing your pink little frost-nipped cheeks, like Thumbelina kissing the little plants outside her burrow good-bye. She saw the swallow coming back at the last minute before she arrived at the black rat's house. But I know that miracles like that are impossible; impossible, it's only a fairy tale.
>
> (Kangkang in Bryant 1989: 122)

For Kangkang's character, the image of Thumbelina, as it does in Andersen's story, suggests all the horror of being poised on the cusp of innocence and experience, threatened by grossness, by an irreversible movement away from childhood innocence to the horrors of growing up into a sexually mature female – someone to be married for the convenience of materialistic concerns and the demands of society. The image of Kangkang's character's 'inner' child holds out the lure of an impossible fairytale escape, the flight from darkness to the romance of rescue by a swallow/knight and an ethereal marriage with a king 'white and almost transparent, as if he were made of glass' (Andersen 1994: 37).

But it is not only sexuality that is at issue in Kangkang's (Persephone-like) use of the Thumbelina motif and perhaps this sends a light backward to illuminate another aspect of Andersen's tale, for it is the materialism of socially approved but loveless marriage that Lu Qinqin despises and ultimately runs away from. Both Andersen and Kangkang, explore the social pressure for material advancement that a judicious but loveless (passion-fearing) marriage can procure.

My earlier psychoanalytic reading of Andersen's tale proposes a sexual conundrum based around collective archetypal content given metaphorical form (chrono-topical 'dress') as body versus an asexual spirit-like 'self' (bridegroom) linked with soul (Thumbelina). It also brings into consciousness shadow images conjoint with a dark and controlling matriarchy. Kangkang's more recent incarnation of the 'Thumbelina' image focuses on the issue of the body as a commodity (whether compliant or under social pressure) in capitalist exchange and the 'inner' child as a symbolic link with past innocence. There is no need for these to be mutually exclusive readings, everything is there in the 'Thumbelina' story for innumerable readings through time and space and there are clear links in the dichotomy between the fragility of the anima and the image of devouring/procuring social mother. What is certain is that there is a propensity in human subjects to visit and revisit the envisioning of archetypes of 'otherness' of 'mothering' of 'relatedness' and that these have become entangled, too, with ever new social pressures and power struggles.

Whether in myths, fairytales or other narratives, manifestations of images such as Andersen's Tömmelise/Thumbelina/Inchelina – call her what you will – have a power that belies the apparent, yet deceptive, simplicity of the vehicles that contain them.

Mopsa

Mopsa, the eponymous protagonist of Jean Ingelow's book *Mopsa the Fairy*, like Thumbelina, arises in miraculous fashion, as a 'nestling' (Ingelow 1912: 4) in a hollow tree, and, as with Thumbelina, a male figure is interposed between the character and readers. Although Ingelow's child character Jack is not the narrator of the story, the narrative is very much focalised through him, with Ingelow's narrator (who refers to Jack as a 'boy, whom I knew very well': Ingelow 1912: 1) offering insights into the boy's thoughts and feelings and recounting events from 'his' perspective. For example, when Jack discovers a nest containing Mopsa and her siblings, the narrator reports: 'He saw that a good way above his head there was a nest – rather a curious one too . . . made of fine white wool and delicate bits of moss . . . like a goldfinch's nest magnified three times' (Ingelow 1912: 2).

This focalisation through Jack rather than Mopsa (the fairy being always enigmatic and distanced from readers) suggests that, symbolically, Jack's journey can be interpreted as if he, metaphorically functioning in fairytale patterning as the ego-hero within the text, penetrates, into the realms of the unconscious, as he is carried through air, on the back of a female albatross, and by river, in a 'beautiful little open boat' (Ingelow 1912: 17), toward distant fairylands. The journey alternates between periods of dreaming and periods when Ingelow's character has surreal adventures in countries bordering the river and on the river itself. There are suggestions that such a journey can be a journey through time, particularly suggestive of a return to the collective unconscious:

> 'Because,' said Mopsa, 'when the albatross brought you, she did not fly with you a long way off, but a long way back – hundreds and hundreds of years. This is your world, as you can see; but none of your people are here, because they are not made yet. I don't think any of them will be made for a thousand years.'
>
> (Ingelow 1912: 117)

In a nineteenth-century world struggling to reconcile Darwinism (*Origin of the Species* was published in 1859) with religious belief, such an image of fairyland is one which draws together fantasy and real, inner and outer 'realities' of body and spirit and soul.

Throughout the journey there are bipolar images, with shadow manifestations at every turn. Jenny, the albatross, is a maternal figure in bird form:

> 'My name,' continued the albatross, 'is Jenny. Do you think you shall remember that? because when you are in Fairyland and want some one to take you home again, and call "Jenny," I shall be able to come to you; and I shall come with pleasure for I like boys better than fairies.'
>
> (Ingelow 1912: 11)

Her counterpart, in the form of a raven, is a devouring female:

> Jack was so thrown off his guard that he snatched one fairy out, [the tiny fairies are in Jack's pockets] just to make sure that it was safe. It was the one with the moustache; and alas! in one instant the raven flew at it, got it out of his hand, and pecked off its head before it had time to wake or Jack to rescue it. Then, as she slowly rose, she croaked, and said to Jack, 'You'll catch it for this, my young master!' and she flew to the bough of a tree, where she finished eating the fairy, and threw his empty little coat into the river.
>
> On this Jack began to cry bitterly, and to think what a foolish boy he had been.
>
> (Ingelow 1912: 40)

Less dramatically, the Queen of Fairies, despite being grateful to Jack for rescuing her, is created by Ingelow as autocratic, proud and jealous of Mopsa. By contrast, her mortal counterpart, the apple-woman, is warm, motherly and supportive of Mopsa and

Jack. Perhaps more significantly, Jack's role casts him as a surrogate 'mother' figure to the young fairies, particularly to his (perhaps) anima, Mopsa, so that it is as if the ego partakes of the maternal sphere and through this learns to love the 'otherness' that is his anima. In this role his successes (the three fairies that survive) and failures (the fairy who dies because Jack is tricked by the raven) metaphorically show both positive and negative 'motherly' care residing in the character. This apparently unusual alliance of the maternal with male ego, is a recurrent feature of miniature literature.[19] At a personal and socio-cultural level, this may demonstrate the desire experienced by some writers to find a way to encourage young readers to bridge a perceived gulf between their culture's constructions of 'masculine' and 'feminine' spheres. It may, however, also express a metaphorical image of ego and mother so close as to be undifferentiated, being drawn together by that aspect of Mopsa which may give expression to the child motif.

As an alliance of child archetype and anima in a single image, Mopsa grows from a tiny creature that Jack can carry in his waistcoat pocket, through engaging baby to fully grown female and Queen: 'now Mopsa had got a crown and a robe and she was so beautiful that Jack thought he should never be tired of looking at her' (Ingelow 1912: 141). Jack's connectedness to her is consistently portrayed as a loving relationship, moving from motherly care to a glimpse of an erotic attachment. It evolves from the first kiss that makes her different from the other fairies – he tells the Fairy Queen that 'I took them out, and laid them in a row, to see if they were safe, and this little one I kissed, because she looked such a little dear' (Ingelow 1912: 88) – to the last moments when it breaks his heart to leave her and give up this highly symbolic journey to return to the world, the home, the mother and the father, Ingelow casts as her character's external reality.

There is much to support the idea of Ingelow's dream-like adventure as engaging, symbolically in an inner rather than outer journey. Not least is the episode when Jack's dreams conjure all manner of frightening creatures, including the Craken, who tells the boy that he must swim his boat to shore under the arches formed by its serpentine coils:

> he looked and saw down the river rainbow behind rainbow – I mean coil behind coil – glittering in the sun, like so many glorious arches that did not reach to the banks, he felt extremely glad

> that this was a dream, and besides that, he thought to himself, 'It's only a fabled monster.' ... The thirtieth coil brushed Jack's cap off, then they [Jack and Mopsa] had to stoop to pass under the two next, and then they had to lie down in the bottom of the boat, and still they got through with the greatest difficulty; but still before them was another! ... When Jack saw it, he called out, 'No! that I cannot bear. Somebody else may do the rest of this dream. I shall jump overboard!'
>
> (Ingelow 1912: 122–3)

In the metaphorical adventure, Jack, as ego-hero, is not ready to engage with his 'shadow', it is only when Mopsa awakens Jack that the monsters of the unconscious vanish, yet 'awake' he remains in the fairylands with still further to travel alongside his rapidly growing Queen-in-waiting.

As with all narratives there can be no definitive, 'for all time' interpretation. The symbolic content 'speaks' to individual readers, stimulating image formation, whether they are the nineteenth-century children Ingelow envisages in her text or the children or adults of later times. Drawing, for the moment, on reader-response theories and the idea of the 'implied reader',[20] as put forward by narratologists such as Seymour Chatman, it seems likely that Ingelow's text is addressed to young boy readers, who may identify with the character, Jack. At a conscious level, the implied author of the work can be seen to encourage this implied male readership to act with kindness toward those, whether animal or human, that are vulnerable and to engage in a warm and protective way with small children and 'worthy' females. Jack is portrayed as being anxious to ensure that Mopsa is cleanly and appropriately clothed, that she is taught to read, and as feeling entirely responsible for her – a duty of care imposed by love and his charge's perceived vulnerability. Throughout the majority of the story, his actions appear thoughtful and kind: he saves and frees the slave he thinks is an old woman; he rescues the fairies imprisoned in parrots' bodies; he helps Mopsa to flee the destiny set out for her by the Fairy Queen. All of these actions point the way toward 'adulthood' for young male readers. Yet there are undercurrents that become more visible if looking at symbolic content and at whether the fairytale moves toward individuation (as suggested in general terms by von Franz (1996) in *The Interpretation of Fairy Tales*).

Ahead of lifting the cover to discover content, the title speaks to a young female readership, drawing female children in with Mopsa's name and promises of fairyland. For readers identifying with Mopsa (and for the female storyteller who tries to focus upon Jack, yet sets the tiny girl-child as ego-hero in her title), it is altogether possible to experience Jack as metaphorical animus – first as a paternal manifestation and second as potential erotic other in the form of his fairy 'twin'. Looking at the tale revisioned in this way, what may lie beneath the surface of 'Mopsa's' story?

Mopsa's travels begin when she is plucked from her nest by Jack:

> His eyes were not used yet to the dim light; but he was sure those things were not birds – no. He poked them and they took no notice; but when he snatched one of them out of the nest, it gave a loud squeak, and said, 'O don't, Jack!' as plainly as possible, upon which he was so frightened that he lost his footing, dropped the thing and slipped down himself.
>
> (Ingelow 1912: 3)

From then until she becomes Queen of her own lands, her being is submerged in Jack. She is hidden in his pockets, her growth is only possible through his care and his kiss, the mortal kiss that makes her different from the other fairies, her siblings (see earlier discussion). She is in his dreams. It is only when she reaches maturity, arriving at the castle where she is destined to be Queen, that she can return Jack's kiss and close her castle gates to leave him to return to his own time and place. If she is a metaphorical vision of child archetype and ego-hero, her early experience of the 'other' of animus is overwhelming – but she acquiesces to 'Old Mother Fate', the unseen 'wise old woman' within the story, in accepting the duty of being Queen to an alien fairy people and to having Jack's fairy double, destined to be the King, as consolation in the kingdom. The castle and crown may well be symbolic of the 'self', with Mopsa moving from paternal animus toward erotic 'other', in the form of the King-to-be (significantly he is created with the same appearance as Jack), as she enters own domain.

There is, however, an epilogue to the book; one that could, perhaps, suggest that the metaphorical 'self' in Ingelow's text may be envisioned as the Christ figure. There are no choices for Mopsa, beyond a duty to 'her' people and acquiescence to a pre-chosen male partner; by extension, the same is true for the girl child outside the book who identifies with the fairy. All is clearly implied in the poem

Ingelow pens for Jack's mother to read, which suggests that the duty imposed upon Ingelow's ego-child, Mopsa, should be read as symbolic of a future mother's duty, giving herself to nurturing her chosen 'flock' and answerable only to the Christ figure, the 'shepherd lord' (Ingelow 1912: 207):

> On Sunny slopes, ah! Long the lady
> Feedeth her flock at noon;
> She leads them down to drink at eve
> Where the small rivulets croon.
> All night her locks are wet with dew,
> Her eyes outwatch the moon.
>
> Over the hills her voice is heard,
> She sings when light doth wane:
> 'My longing heart is full of love.
> When shall my loss be gain?
> My shepherd lord, I see him not,
> But he will come again.'
>
> (Ingelow 1912: 207)

Afterword to Part I

At this stage, although I have pointed toward possible interpretations of the content that may underlay simple miniature characters in fairytales, it would be entirely wrong to give these ideas the status of conclusions. In this part of the book I have been looking toward what may be revealed by exploring fairytale-style story characters as expressions of collective archetypal content and have been concerned to suggest or show what may be the first and simplest 'dress' of these as they appear as proto-characters. I have included as much detail about the characters as possible, so that *my* readers may, in turn, have the opportunity of making their own readings from the (in my view) rich material that lies within tales such as those I have examined.

Certain aspects, however, seem to force their way to the forefront of my thinking, particularly the way in which certain gender-role-related patterns and relationships emerge through the metaphorical expression of archetypal alliances, both those compressed within any individual image and those expressed in the miniature character's 'relationships' with surrounding figures.

In the early English versions, the male miniature Tom Thumb clearly links ego-hero with trickster and separates, vigorously and repetitiously, from the primal bodily maternal. Prior (to the 1621 text) mention of the character in connection with certain episodes and the pictorial renderings of some of these in later woodcuts and engravings all attest to the robustness of much of the matter of the first segment of the 1621 tale.[21] Beyond this, in the story in which Tom Thumb survives, 'his' anima is conceived as a spiritual, nurturing goddess-like figure, linked with magical gifts (including shape-shifting ability) and with the legendary King Arthur, as the manikin puts aside 'his' hyperbolic shadow and emerges into maturity. In the story in which the manikin dies, 'his' anima is given image as the tabooed erotic 'other', the Queen.

In the Japanese story there is no such robust repetition of any tricksterish alliance or resistance toward the female as maternal body or erotic 'other'. Female–male connectedness forms a pattern across the story. There is the mother–father dyad, from which, under the aegis of a god-like figure, the third, the manikin, springs. In narrative terms the character achieves separation from parental figures in a way that is depicted as natural and non-traumatic. Equally flawlessly achieved, within the metaphorical subtext of the story, is the joining of ego-hero and princess anima. There is, in other words, a continual metaphorical expression of balance and harmony between male subject and 'soul-image' (perhaps a narrative pattern that gives another 'dress' to the conjoint yinyang symbol originating in Taoist philosophy). The encounter with the shadow, imagined in the form of evil spirits, is in company with the anima, and, ultimately, the ego-hero, conjoint with divine child, arises as a new mature-figure (metaphorically expressed in growth to adult size), through possession of the wish-giving mallet.

The stories have apparently similar characters, but very different 'dress'. Whether metaphorical expression of anima or minute female ego-hero, the Scandinavian miniature, Tömmelise, and the English fairy, Mopsa, have no alliances with images of the trickster; there is, on the other hand, everything to suggest that within them there is also a metaphorical representation of the motif of maiden, the Kore (see discussion in Part II of Jung's and Kerényi's *Essays on a Science of Mythology*). Yet even in this apparent division from the Tom Thumb character they are alike in the sense of separation from all expression of earthly union with 'other' (this time envisioned in male form). The movement is away from mythical Persephone's underworld ravisher and toward a male figure that is not part of the Persephone myth, but may well be an expression of a Christ-like figure. From the image of an innocent child, through the trials of a beleaguered maiden, the dynamics of these characters seem to speak, in Jungian terms, to the idea of a perpetuating cycle of anima or ego as proto-madonna in union with the God 'self'. What is particularly significant here is that this 'dress' to patterns of individuation is the envisioning of both female and male consciousnesses in the persons of Ingelow and Andersen.

As a postscript to these case studies, I have looked at two further examples of English Victorian productions which feature fairytale characters, with the idea of seeing the extent to which there may be any repetition of the alliances and relationships mentioned above. In the first of these, a female writer, Christina Rossetti, envisions fantasy male figures which take the form of semi-theriomorphic goblins in her poem *Goblin Market*.[22] As I suggest in Chapter 1, the poem has ambivalent status in terms of implied audience: is it a fairytale poem for children or a fantasy poem for adults, replete with sexual symbolism, or both (Carpenter and Prichard 1995: 209)? By way of background to the writing of the poem, Frances Thomas (in her biography of Christina Rossetti) suggests that it was written shortly after a period of time during which Rossetti *may* have been suffering from 'depression . . . manifest in psychotic symptoms, delusions of damnation combined with a sense of worthlessness and despair' (Thomas 1994: 178).

Goblin Market is a tale, in verse, of two sisters, Laura and Lizzie, who are beset by the temptation to try the enchanted and alluring fruits offered by mysterious and magical goblin strangers:

> 'Look Lizzie, look Lizzie,
> Down the glen tramp little men.
> One hauls a basket,
> One bears a plate,
> One lugs a golden dish
> Of many pounds' weight.
> How fair the vine must grow
> Whose grapes are so luscious;
> How warm the wind must blow
> Through those fruit bushes.'
> 'No,' said Lizzie: 'No, no, no;
> Their offers should not charm us,
> Their evil gifts would harm us.'
> She thrust a dimpled finger
> In each ear shut eyes and ran:
> Curious Laura chose to linger
> Wondering at each merchant man.
> (Rossetti 1939: 10–11)

Lizzie runs, Laura succumbs, and all the payment ostensibly required of her is a lock of hair:

She clipped a precious golden lock,
She dropped a tear more rare than pearl,
Then sucked their fruit globes fair or red:
Sweeter that honey from the rock,
Stronger that man-rejoicing wine,
Clearer than water flowed that juice;
She never tasted such before,
. . .
She sucked until her lips were sore;
Then flung the emptied rinds away
But gathered up one kernel-stone,
And knew not was it night or day
As she turned home alone.
(Rossetti 1939: 15–16)

The cruelty of the goblin men is then revealed: they and their wares become invisible to Laura, but she is left with an unending craving for more, and, unable to fulfil her longing to taste again, falls first into rage and then into death-presaging lethargy. At this point, Lizzie, despairing of her sister, who is 'knocking at Death's door' (26), visits the goblin men, whose voices she alone now hears and, in a rape-reminiscent scene:

They trod and hustled her,
Elbowed and jostled her,
Clawed with their nails,
Barking, mewing, hissing, mocking,
Tore her gown and soiled her stocking,
Twitched her hair out by the roots,
Stamped upon her tender feet,
Held her hands and squeezed their fruits
Against her mouth to make her eat.
[. . . Lizzie resists]
Like a royal virgin town
Topped with gilded dome and spire
Close beleaguered by a fleet
Mad to tug her standard down.
(Rossetti 1939: 29–30)

In the end, Lizzie, though preventing the fruits from passing her lips, has enough of the juice on her mouth and skin to allow Laura another orgy, this time taking the juices from her sister, as she 'kisse[. . .s] and kisse[. . .s] her with a hungry mouth' (33). The juices are transformed into 'wormwood to her tongue' and, sated, Laura falls unconscious to the ground. In a passage clearly speaking to ideas of rebirth, readers learn that the crisis has passed and that Laura is restored.

> Life out of death.
> . . .
> But when the first birds chirped about their eaves,
> And early reapers plodded to the place
> Of golden sheaves,
> And dew-wet grass
> Bowed in the morning winds so brisk to pass,
> And the new buds with new day
> Opened of cup-like lilies on the stream,
> Laura awoke as from a dream
> (Rossetti 1939: 35)

I have quoted at considerable length from the poem, for it is the language in which it is written more than the storyline in bald terms that creates a vivid impression of Rossetti's fantasy vision.

There are innumerable possible symbolic readings of *Goblin Market*, from an interpretation of the poem as extreme erotic fantasy (Duffy quoted in Thomas 1996: 170) to the idea of it being 'a story of redemption through sacrifice' (Thomas 1996: 175). (Thomas suggests that this would have been a contemporary view.) For me, in exploring the poem as visionary fantasy, there is much to suggest that it symbolises an inward journey for Rossetti's protagonists rather than an outer adventure. It is as if the girls represent female ego-hero (and maiden) split into two: the cautious and morally 'good' aspect taking form as Lizzie (perhaps Persephone above ground) and the 'shadow' temptation-ridden aspect taking form as Laura (perhaps Persephone in the underworld). The shadow points the way to an encounter with animus in trickster alliance as Laura orgiastically encounters the goblin men. Lizzie, ultimately, must follow, but 'she' resists being overwhelmed and there is no union between these compelling and dangerous forces. The sisters, though, are reunited, and, metaphorically, the sexual energy of the shadow is defused, 'other' is somehow defeated with the ego repressing all trace of animus as the goblin men, thwarted, are vanquished:

> Some writhed on the ground,
> Some dived into the brook
> With ring and ripple,
> Some scudded on the gale without a sound,
> Some vanished in the distance.
>
> (Rossetti 1939: 31)

It is as if the collective content manifest in the Persephone myth, and envisioned in Rossetti's tale as the maiden Lizzie/Laura, is denied all contact with 'poisonous' 'masculinity'. The ego resists the unconscious and is envisioned, in itself, enacting the sacrifice necessary to achieve an ego/madonna unity in a single vision of female unity held with an iron-grip on the edge of the unconscious abyss. Tricksterish masculinity is again the victim of the 'dressing' of this tale, as is the 'shadow' sexual energy associated with a female subject – Tom Thumb and Tömmelise all over again.

In another dimension, that of the art world, the Victorian fairy painting genre offers striking examples of the 'child' motif in fairy form. Here an envisioning of 'shadow' seems to dominate the imagination of painters such as Richard Dadd (see p. 24), where the tiniest image may speak to a fantasy world of sexual excess, cruelty and perversion. Dadd's fantastic portrayals may owe something to his own mental health problems – the artist was confined in Bethlem Hospital (Bedlam) and later in Broadmoor after murdering his father (reportedly believing that it was not his father, but a devil that had taken on his father's form[23]) – but there were many others who painted similar subject matter. If Dadd's image of *Puck* (see cover) can be read as a conjoint image of shadow and divine child given form as the demonic naked baby, John Anster Fitzgerald's *The Fairy's Lake* offers an equally demonic (conjoint shadow-trickster perhaps) figure in the form of a bulge-eyed, flaming-haired, open-mouthed goblin descending with lance on a bathing fairy maiden, the latter highlighted in sparklingly light paint and depicted as horribly vulnerable, with partially submerged wings.[24] The existence of many images, emanating from Victorian artists such as Richard Dadd, Richard Doyle, John Anster Fitzgerald, Thomas Heatherley and others, images that speak to an engagement with supernatural forms enacting patterns that seem to have emerged from the shadow of the unconscious, is, in itself, interesting – that these should take shape as child-sized figures throws a strange and contrary light on the didactic literature produced for real, living, breathing children in Victorian times (see Chapter 1). Perhaps images of the repressed 'wild' and sexually available child from the adult unconscious must occasionally break free in some form of overt expression.

Part II

Foreword to Part II

Moving on from the Victorian era and looking at later miniature literature from the twentieth century, the kind of character formations I point toward in Chapter 1 begin to emerge. Here there are characters that are more complex than those of fairytale, in the sense of appearing as single figures but holding multiple strands in tension within them. On the one hand, there is still a suggestion of collective content in what appear to be archetypal images, as envisioned by writers and illustrators and drawn forward from fairytale, myth and legend. On the other, it is clear that such elements are overlaid with a 'classic realist' simulation of thinking, feeling, dreaming 'real' children.

The 'classic realist' tendency in children's literature is evident throughout the twentieth century (see discussion on pp. 16–17, drawing on, in particular, Rose 1984) and its use in miniature literature creates an immediate tension between fantasy and realism. Adult writers create heroes and child readers are, potentially, drawn in through identification with or empathy for an 'other' (the adult-created child) that pretends not to be. A fascinatingly smooth surface pool promises underlying cross-currents that may reveal much about adults and the 'child that haunts us'.

To look at material from throughout the twentieth century is not feasible in terms of time and word constraints. Instead I have chosen to concentrate, largely, on what I regard as a 'hotspot' for possible tension. I am referring to a period that encompasses the end of the Second World War and the so-called 'Cold War' that followed on from this.

Looking back to that period of time it is clear that in the aftermath of the Second World War, humanity was faced with coming to terms with a twofold grim knowledge: awareness of the extent to which the shadow-side of the human psyche could manifest in actions as terrible as those perpetrated by humankind on humankind, and awareness that the technologies unleashed could not be put 'back in the box' and, indeed, were likely to multiply and intensify in harmful potential. In such a time and place it is scarcely surprising that a requestioning of what it is to be human could find form in a new eruption of the child motif, perhaps in response to a deep-felt need for re-engagement with an imagined past innocence and hopes for the rebirth of the child image of futurity in the form of a 'saviour' figure.

The domain of children's literature is a natural arena for such an appearance to find form, being a place where adult writers (and disseminators of literature for children) might imagine the possibility of influencing real children (and thus the future). Yet, paradoxically, the domain also represents an arena in which adult writers can engage (whether consciously or unconsciously) in inner confrontation with a sense of a collective 'shadow', returning to the symbolic 'child', hidden beneath the simulated 'real' child. The symbolic child, in Jung's view, is capable of simultaneously 'existing' in the moment of its appearance while speaking to pre-conscious beginnings *and* pointing the way to the future (Jung in Jung and Kerényi 1963: 79–83). For adult writers of the period, perhaps, the symbolic child could speak to a rebirth and a revisioning of a maturation pattern that might enable the human psyche to survive in the shadows of genocide and nuclear horror.

In David Tacey's discussion of 'The Underground God' (2006), he suggests that:

> Ultimate reality is seen [by Jung] as an interplay of conflicting forces, *yin* and *yang*, darkness and light. Because Western religion has viewed God as yang and masculine (Father and Son), there has been a damming up of the energies that have been left out of the picture. With the collapse of the traditional image of God, the time is right for the release of yin aspects of the divine. These aspects include instinct, sexuality and the so-called 'dark side', and could never have emerged unless the official image had collapsed.
>
> (Tacey 2006: 42)

In my case studies in Part II it will be interesting to see whether there are any early signs of the emergence of 'instinct, sexuality and the so-called “dark side”’ and the extent to which this harmonises or conflicts with the role models that are consciously constructed and put forward for child readers to imbibe and emulate.

Chapter 4

Odysseys and the Motherland

Before moving into the post-Second-World-War period I want to introduce, for comparative purposes, a text by the 1909 winner of the Nobel Prize in Literature, Selma Lagerlöf. *Nils Holgerssons Underbara Resa Genom Sverige* was published in two parts in 1906 and 1907, and the story makes a useful comparison with two English books by 'BB' (Denys Watkins-Pitchford): *The Little Grey Men* (first published during the Second World War in 1942) and its sequel *The Little Grey Men Go Down the Bright Stream* (first published in the immediate post-war period in 1948). The miniature protagonists in both Lagerlöf's and 'BB's' texts are involved in epic journeys, making their stories ideal to compare in order to see whether similar content arises from the depths of each of the tales – tales which are also of eco-critical interest, being vitally concerned with the landscape and the natural world, despite being published around forty years apart.

Nils Holgersson

At the start of Lagerlöf's story (translated into English from the original Swedish by Lagerlöf's friend, Velma Swanston Howard, as *The Wonderful Adventures of Nils* and *Further Adventures of Nils*), her protagonist Nils Holgersson is presented as a full-sized boy character, the despair of his mother, who, Lagerlöf's omniscient narrator advises, was 'distressed because he was wild and bad, cruel to animals, and ill tempered toward human beings' (Lagerlöf 1950: 3). The mother's prayer to God to effect some change in her son begins to be answered in an unexpected way, when the boy, trying to cheat an elf he has captured, is himself turned by the elf into a 'little, little creature' (Lagerlöf 1950: 8):

> Nils ran round the glass several times, to see if there wasn't a little man hidden behind it, but he found no one there; and then he began to shake with terror. For now he understood that the elf had bewitched him, and that the creature whose image he saw in the glass was he, himself.
>
> (Lagerlöf 1950: 9)

This is the start of the fantasy part of the tale, as the protagonist, transformed into elf-like creature, is able to take wing, on the back of the homestead's domesticated goose (Morten Goosey-Gander) and together they journey north, experiencing many adventures on the way, in the company of a flock of wild geese.

At its simplest level Lagerlöf's narrative is a vehicle for a moral tale which has the added purpose of acquainting child readers with the geography and folklore of Lagerlöf's homeland. The foreword to the 1950 edition explains that the National Teachers' Association of Sweden asked her to write a 'geographical reader' for Swedish children and adds that Lagerlöf spent a number of years drawing together material relating to both the natural history and the folkloric history of the individual (and very different) Swedish provinces (Lagerlöf 1950: v).

The book follows this remit faithfully. The tiny boy (frequently linked with the Tom Thumb character by his nickname 'Tummetott', which a footnote advises is the 'Swedish word for Tom Thumb': Lagerlöf 1950: 11) reforms, immeasurably, in moral character (in terms of caring for the welfare of – and loving – others, including wildlife) during his epic flight north; at the same time, his fictional journey allows each province of Sweden to be described and commented upon as he travels over and on Lagerlöf's homeland. Yet this is far more than a textbook with a story and a moral dimension.

Inside the world of Lagerlöf's fiction is a tiny child, both akin to the child motif made apparent in the metaphorical form of a 'Tom Thumb' and, simultaneously, the writer's conscious creation of a thinking, feeling, child-alike consciousness. Lagerlöf, through her narrator's voice and the character's words, ensures that readers are aware of Nils' every hope, fear, joy and sorrow, in a manner that suggests the presence of a recognisably 'real' child. Child readers are given an adventurous hero to identify with, but the story also charts a journey of moral growth. At the start of the tale, the narrator conveys the boy's alienation from feelings of love and responsibility. Readers see examples of the cruel 'jokes' the full-sized Nils plays on the animals on the homestead and are told in words that he loves and respects no one, neither parents, peers nor teachers. Through episodic revelations, as the protagonist begins to gain the trust and respect of his companions, examples of his behaviour and narratorially controlled accounts of 'his' thought processes, chart a gradually dawning change from wild and uncaring boy into a thoughtful, loving and responsible individual.

In the surface tale, the leader of the flock of wild geese, the anthropomorphised 'mother' Akka, gives wise counsel and example to the boy and he, in turn, learns to love and respect her. He is instrumental in saving her from the savage Smirre Fox, who continually harries and preys on the geese. (Nils saves the geese and other wildlife at various points in the story and they, in turn, do all that is in their power to protect him as part of a supportive community.) When Smirre Fox offers the geese the promise of security in exchange for 'Tummetott's' life, having set otter and marten to attack and harass them as they try to rest, the response is a significant one:

> Smirre thought that Akka sounded scared, and he said quickly: 'If you, Akka, will take that Tummetott – who has so often opposed me – and throw him down to me, I'll promise to make peace with you. Then I'll never more pursue you or any of yours.'
>
> 'I'm not going to give you Tummetott,' said Akka. 'From the youngest of us to the oldest, we would willingly give our lives for his sake!'
>
> 'Since you're so fond of him,' said Smirre, 'I'll promise you that he shall be the first among you that I will wreak vengeance upon.'
>
> Akka said no more, and after Smirre had sent up a few more barks, all was still. Nils lay all the while awake. Now it was Akka's words to the fox that prevented him from sleeping. Never had he dreamed that he should hear anything so great as that any one was willing to risk life for his sake. From that moment it could no longer be said of Nils Holgersson that he did not care for any one.
>
> (Lagerlöf 1950: 133)

Yet within the fiction too is the storyteller's voice, framing the tale, a voice that readers are intended to understand as Lagerlöf's own voice, for, like Andersen, she claims her own status as teller of the tale, dreamer of the fantastical events. In a metafictional moment she tells of her initial inability to create the story which is the very one her words appear in. Casting herself as 'a woman who thought of writing a book about Sweden which would be suitable for children' (Lagerlöf 1930: 294), Lagerlöf speaks of her initial lack of inspiration and despair of writing a book that must be factual rather than the fiction that is her usual creative output. But at last she recounts, in emotional – even spiritual – terms, a tale of her return to her old home (which had been sold, many years earlier, on the death of her father):

> She lingered in the shadow under the big mountain-ash at the entrance to the farm, and stood looking about her. As she stood there a strange thing happened; a flock of doves came and lit beside her.
>
> She could hardly believe that they were real birds, for doves are not in the habit moving about after sundown. . . . Perhaps her father had sent his birds with a greeting to her, so that she would not feel so sad and lonely when she came to her former home. As she thought of this there welled up within her such an intense longing for the old times that her eyes filled with tears. . . .
>
> 'Won't you fly to father and tell him that I long to come home? I have wandered long enough in strange places. Ask him if he can't arrange it so that I may soon turn back to my childhood's home.'
>
> The moment she had said this the flock of doves rose and flew away. She tried to follow them with her eyes, but they vanished instantly. It was as if the whole white company had dissolved in the shimmering air.
>
> (Lagerlöf 1930: 300–2)

Fantasy and reality are mixed in this account of a numinous moment; there is more than a suggestion that, for the implied author of the work, an inner vision of a wise old man, in the image of her own dead father, mediated by the doves, is experienced as a guiding presence at this moment in her life.[25] It is here in this account (which occurs late in the book) of a writer's homecoming, whether fictional, factual or mixture of the two, that the miniature Nils is 'introduced' to the writer-in-the-book who subsequently tells 'his' tale and allows him to transport her, metaphorically, through air and on land throughout the length and breadth of her own homeland.

Moments after the doves have disappeared into the night, she sees 'a tiny midget, no taller than a hand's breadth, struggling with a brown owl' (Lagerlöf 190: 303). Needless to say, the writer-as-character effects his rescue and is rewarded with 'his' story and the inspiration for hers.

In this creative work, the tiny child, interpreted within the text as being sent by the dead father as a sign, shows the way for the writer-as-character to penetrate, metaphorically, into the landscape of her homeland and its collective spirit, to take wing with the wild geese, to encounter the savagery of Smirre Fox and, ultimately, to accommodate all this in the hero's return. At the end of the tale – with its mysterious provenance as manikin's 'true' tale and writer's vision, with embedded retellings of folktales and legends from the birth of the land – the tiny child is reborn in human form in the parental home; a young man arising spontaneously from the manikin. The symbolic significance of this from the perspective of a reader following Lagerlöf's journey is the penetration of layers of local context (Lagerlöf's chrono-topical and personal moment – her need and desire to set down a sense of Sweden, its history, geography, peoples, and her need and desire to return to the homestead of her childhood) to deeper collective content, in the alliance of Lagerlöf's tale with the undercurrents of folklore and legends of the land.

In his presentation speech, on the occasion of Lagerlöf's acceptance of the Nobel Prize in Literature, Claes Annerstedt (1909) suggests that:

> the realm of her [Lagerlöf's] true heritage . . . [is] the mystical world of fairy tales and legends. Only a soul that had fed on legends since the days of childhood, and that added love to a rich imagination, could dare to interpret the secrets of the invisible world that the visionary always sees beside or rather beneath the visible world. The visionary quality that is so characteristic in Lagerlöf's writings has been stronger in her than in anyone since the days of St. Birgitta.
>
> (Annerstedt 1909)

Annerstedt links 'the mystical world of fairy tales and legends' to Lagerlöf's 'soul' and a 'visionary quality' in her writings, and, in turn, this aligns with Jung's account of visionary literature in 'Psychology and Literature' in *The Spirit in Man Art and Literature* (particularly *CW* 15: 133–54). In her writings, Lagerlöf engages with outer realities and personal and inner visions arising from both her personal and the collective unconscious. Jung continually draws attention to the importance of the creative arts in dreaming, anew, images for the mythic figures and patterns that speak to the mysteries of the unconscious through the ages. As Tacey (2006) suggests:

> In this work of updating and translating [myth] the role of the arts is crucial, as Jung realized (*CW* 15). Depth psychology, he believed, must work in tandem with the creative arts, whose task is to revive the ancient figures and forces. Both the artist and the psychologist realise the necessity of 'making new' the ancient truths that have become opaque and obscure in our time.
>
> (Tacey 2006: 22)

The possibility of a visionary dimension to her work is acknowledged by Lagerlöf in her Nobel acceptance speech as she remembers an imaginary conversation with her father, arising in the fashion of a waking dream on a long train journey, when:

> All rustle and bustle cease and the sound of the wheels becomes a soothing, peaceful melody. The coaches no longer seem to run on rails and sleepers but glide into space. Well, that is how it was as I sat there and thought how much I should like to see my old father again. So light and soundless was the movement of the train that I could hardly imagine I was on this earth. And so I began to daydream.
>
> (Lagerlöf 1909)[26]

In her remembered account of this 'daydream', Lagerlöf tells of addressing the vision that appears to her as her dead father, acknowledging her 'debt' as a writer, to her formative experiences that drew the symbolic patterns of folktale and legend deep into her psyche. She speaks of the songs and stories, the fairytales and legends, as her legacy – passed on from

> poor, homeless vagabonds . . . playing the fool and singing all those songs. What do I not owe to them, to their mischief and mad pranks! And the old men and women sitting in their small grey cottages as one came out of the forest, telling me wonderful stories of water-sprites and trolls and enchanted maidens lured into the mountains. It was they who taught me that there is

> poetry in hard rocks and black forests. . . . And I am in debt not only to people; there is the whole of nature as well. The animals that walk the earth, the birds in the skies, the trees and flowers, they have all told me some of their secrets.
>
> (Lagerlöf 1909)

So the character of Nils seems to be both consciously and unconsciously conceived in a meld of realistically created child consciousness and metaphorical divine child – sometimes the trickster, more often the hero and, perhaps, even ultimately the 'self' within the text. With such an amalgam it seems entirely possible that there is particular symbolic significance in those story moments where the balance between these incarnations shifts: such as the moment when Nils is transformed from human boy to miniature Tom Thumb-alike creature; the moments when his trickster characteristics are subsumed by his heroic deeds; the moments when he is far more vulnerable than a human child; the moments when he begins to stop to listen and learn from the 'wise old woman' in the form of the goose, Akka; the moment when he is transformed back into a full-size young man.

The moments associated with the parent–child bond seem, potentially, the most significant. Lagerlöf, as writer and as writer-as-character, experiences 'daydream' visions of her dead father and links his appearances with her creative work and with her formative experiences of her homeland, and its wealth of folktale, legend and the natural world, all mediated through the father–daughter bond. Jung, in his essay on 'The Phenomenology of the Spirit in Fairy-tales', speaks to there being what he terms a 'spiritual' dimension to dreams of a father-figure (Jung specifically mentions the dreams of patients with a particular kind of father-complex), a wise old man who offers sage advice to the dreamer (*CW* 9i: 396). In her dream, the writer-as-character is guided by the spirit appearing as her dead father and follows a tiny and vulnerable, possible animus image in manikin form (transformed from a wild and ill-behaved full-sized boy) away from his parental home into a fantasy journey. Later, in the imaginal form of Akka the wild goose, it is the wisdom of a theriomorphic mother (echoes of the mother goose of fairytale provenance) that becomes the respected guide to nature for the writer's imaginative travels. The now-parentless manikin is reborn as the child of the bird-mother and begins a journey which metaphorically penetrates to the depths of the writer's unconscious, as it recounts a flight of fantasy in which topography, history and collective spirit are uncovered.

Beneath the surface tale, despite the presence of the wise old man (the father of Lagerlöf's vision), there is an increasing sense of a natural and eternal maternal in the all-nurturing, yet formidable, Mother Akka, as the wild geese penetrate deeper and deeper into the writer's homeland. Here the infinite cycles of migration and the infinite cycles of birth and death coalesce in a single image that moves beyond the specific character which Lagerlöf creates.

Mother Akka is intimately connected with two episodes where the writer envisions theriomorphic images that draw in a sense of the shadow side of 'otherness'. In these episodes, mothering is conflicted with the natural aggression of eagle and fox – both here represented, significantly, as male.

In the first episode, Nils encounters Gorgo the eagle and learns that he, like Nils, is a foster son of Mother Akka. As an eaglet, Gorgo is orphaned and survives only through Akka's efforts to feed him. The goose takes fish and frogs to the growing bird and later encourages him to fly with the wild geese. But when he strikes a chicken, Akka starts 'beating him with her bill' (Lagerlöf 1930: 162) and, though he submits, the taunts of the other birds drive him into bidding an angry farewell to his saviour/mother:

> The eagle . . . turned toward Akka with flaming eyes, as though he would have liked to attack her. But he suddenly changed his mind, and with quick wing strokes bounded into the air, soaring so high that no call could reach him; and he sailed around up there as long as the wild geese saw him.
>
> Two days later he appeared again in the wild goose flock.
>
> 'I know who I am,' he said to Akka. 'Since I am an eagle, I must live as becomes an eagle; but I think that we can be friends all the same. You or any of yours I shall never attack.'
>
> But Akka had set her heart on successfully training an eagle into a mild and harmless bird and she could not tolerate his wanting to do as he chose.
>
> 'Do you think that I wish to be the friend of bird-eater?' She asked. 'Live as I have taught you to live, and you may travel with my flock as heretofore.'
>
> Both were proud and stubborn, and neither of them would yield. It ended in Akka's forbidding the eagle to show his face in

> her neighbourhood, and her anger toward him was so intense that no one dared speak his name in her presence.
>
> (Lagerlöf 1930: 163)

Later in Lagerlöf's account Nils rescues Gorgo from captivity and from the increasing torpor that has beset the eagle there, a torpor which prevents him from attempting to escape. In his turn Gorgo rescues Nils and returns him to Akka one night, while the wild geese sleep. Before revealing the eagle's presence Nils 'tests' Akka's reaction by telling her that he had seen the imprisoned Gorgo, but was afraid to set him free because of his wild and untameable nature. Akka is angry to think of Gorgo remaining in captivity and when Nils asks if he acted wisely in leaving him there, she retorts: ' "No, it was not right!" . . . "Say what you will about the eagles, they are proud birds and greater lovers of freedom than all others. It is not right to keep them in captivity" ' (Lagerlöf 1930: 240). But Gorgo has not been left to suffer. Through the auspices of the manikin, Akka and her 'wild' foster son are reunited, with Nils' rejoicing, ' "There are those who say that you no longer have any love in your heart for the one you reared so tenderly, because he lives as eagles must live. But I know now that it isn't true" ' (Lagerlöf 1930: 240).

In surface-story terms the protagonist is used to help child readers understand that each creature must live according to its own 'wild' nature and will never flourish in captivity or be bent against its own instinctual life. Akka functions as a 'touchstone' character – her acceptance of Gorgo becomes confirmation of the appropriateness of the child character's action in rescuing the eagle. At a deeper level, it is as though, through the intervention of the 'divine child', accommodation between the archetypal mother and the repressed 'wildness' that is 'other' to her nurturing being is possible.

In a similar incident, Nils also admits to Akka that he has saved the life of Smirre Fox. Readers of the book may find this astonishing, having vicariously experienced the fox's repeated attempts to kill Akka and the boy, and his success at other times in killing birds from the goose flock. Yet Nils is depicted by Lagerlöf as taking pity on his arch enemy, who is imprisoned in a cage at Skansen. The manikin learns that men are coming to take captive foxes to an island, where they are needed to control the rat population and is instrumental in Smirre Fox being chosen. Here too, Akka is shown approving his actions: ' "What say you to this Mother Akka? If you had been in my place, would you not have done likewise?" "You have acted in a way that makes me wish I had done that myself," said the leader-goose proudly"' (Lagerlöf 1930: 239).

For readers, old mother Akka's approval is again the implied authorial 'touchstone' for the ethical 'correctness' of forgiveness. At a deeper level, where the unconscious finds conscious expression in the images created by the writer, the 'child' could be interpreted as pointing a way toward futurity to the archetypal mother in an accommodation, rather than elimination, of 'shadow' aggression and perhaps suggesting that at this level the story symbolically portrays the imaginal projection of the implied author's inner journey, under the aegis of the father spirit, to encounter visions of animus, of wise old woman, of divine child and ultimately the 'self' arising from pre-existing propensities in the collective unconscious.

Readings, however, are limitless – for some, particularly child readers at a stage of reading development in which identification with a protagonist is a predominant mode of narrative engagement (see Appleyard 1994: ch. 2), alternative perspectives are more likely to dominate. There is sufficient of the 'real' child in Lagerlöf's portrayal of 'Nils as hero' to tempt child readers to allow the character to become themselves as reader-in-the-book.

Taking to wing with Nils, in his vulnerable incarnation as miniature boy, readers can be transported into encountering Lagerlöf's vision and, through the medium of narrative empathy, making it their own, as they vicariously experience danger of injury, captivity (portrayed as a kind of death) and death itself, dealt at seeming random from the violence of theriomorphic figures (fox, bear, marten, crow), from starvation, from fire, from falling, from being lost and alone, from humans that would possess and abuse him. Here it is not just an image of the child motif that is condensed and vulnerable but, arguably, the reader's ego. Here it is the reader-in-the-book who is in confrontation with images arising from Lagerlöf's personal and chrono-topical vision of a child's adventures melded with those arising from collective unconscious content, which may in turn stimulate unconscious material to arise from the depths of a reader's own unconscious (see Rowland 1999: 63).

The story moments that seem of most significance in such a reading are those in which the tiny figure is directly involved in relationships with other characters. In particular there are his relationships with 'other' in the form of the wild geese, mother Akka and Dunfin, and his relationships, both caring and combative, with aspects that may be interpreted as versions of 'masculinity' in the male forms of the white domestic gander, Smirre Fox and Gorgo the eagle. The images that are in female form are depicted as wise, authoritative and idealised. Akka has already been discussed in this chapter and needs no further introduction, other than to say that she is portrayed as the leader of the flock, a creature who commands respect from all those (both male and female) around her. Dunfin, the female grey goose who becomes the partner of Nils' white gander, is described in the following terms: 'her feather dress was like soft satin and her eyes were mild and pleading' (Lagerlöf 1950: 160) and the narratorial account of the effect upon Tummetott is startling:

> Occasionally one finds something in animals which makes one wonder what sort of creatures they really are. One is almost afraid that they may be transformed human beings. It was something like this with the grey goose [Dunfin] . . .
>
> 'This surely can't be a bird' thought he [Tummetott.] 'It is certainly some bewitched princess.'
>
> (Lagerlöf 1950: 160–1)

Elsewhere the sentiment is repeated as Dunfin emerges from her morning bath (perhaps even with echoes of Aphrodite emerging from the foam): 'The drops of water lay pearl-dew on her shimmery satin-like feathers, and Tummetott thought once again that she was a real little princess' (Lagerlöf 1950: 162). This is an entrancing fairytale metaphorical image of theriomorphic anima for those readers in an empathic identification with Tummetott to encounter. It also provides a symbol of human integration with nature: the 'real' human child is transformed into the symbolic child on an inner journey – the inner experience of anima is then intimately related to the natural world in the image of Dunfin. In some senses the image arises from an adult writer's own journey; child readers have been lured into focalising everything within the text through the conjoined simulated 'real' *and* metaphorical child. Yet the fairytale aspect of the text still dresses archetypal propensities for readers in the 'time-spirit' of Lagerlöf's chrono-topical moment. Dunfin/anima is clearly linked with female patterns from the fairytale tradition. As the passive and suffering princess, she has jealous sisters, who try to destroy her prince (the white gander) in a reiteration of the sibling jealousies so frequently portrayed in fairytales such as the 'Cinderella' and 'Beauty and the Beast' type tales:

> Dunfin had two sisters, Prettywing and Goldeye. They were strong and intelligent birds, but they did not have such a soft and shiny feather dress as Dunfin, nor did they have her sweet and gentle disposition. From the time they had been little, yellow goslings, their parents and relatives and even the old fisherman had plainly showed them that they thought more of Dunfin than of them, Therefore the sisters had always hated her.
>
> (Lagerlöf 1930: 122)

Regardless of whether a psychoanalytical-critical reading of Nils' narrative function may regard 'his' symbolic core as that of animus, divine child or ego-hero, or mix of these, this is a text in which wisdom and fortitude are consciously presented as having value, as are kindness, and bravery in pursuit of the good of others. Love and forgiveness are all given form within the figures of Akka and her foster children, in Morten Goosey-Gander and Dunfin.

It is also a text in which both the natural world, in all its vital, living incarnations, and the communities who build upon and cultivate that land are valued. The instinctual and natural are given imaginal form. Whether the fox and the eagle, fulfilling their need to kill other creatures, are anthropomorphised in terms of motivation, or, conversely, are theriomorphic embodiments of a collective inner shadow steeped in necessary violence and death, readers are still brought to the same point in terms of the text as a communicative medium.

Death happens randomly in Lagerlöf's account: Osa the goose-girl loses her mother and even her last sibling to illness and accident; an old woman dies alone, never again seeing her children and grandchildren, who have moved to a new land; geese die on the annual flight north; the 'wise' crow saves Tummetott and regains his leadership of the crow flock only to perish in his hour of triumph. On the other hand, for no other reason than the intervention of the hero (and there is more than a little suggestion of the boy as a saviour figure as the story progresses), working with the help of others, a little boy is saved from drowning, vital bird habitat is preserved, geese survive attack, wild creatures are freed from captivity – for readers, the randomness of both ill and good 'luck' and the inevitability of death are all shown as ever-present aspects of life. Beyond this, the natural world and the inhabitants of the land are linked with the patterning of myth, legend and fairytale in the traditional stories that Lagerlöf chooses to relate in conjunction with each real Swedish province portrayed on Nils' fantasy journey. The whole suggests a futurity in the conjoining of instinct and reason, nature and humankind, inner unconscious and outer consciousness, through the figure of the child who embodies all these in his elf and human incarnations.

In its depths, the tale is not only the fairy-tale account of an individual, but also the story of individuals blending into communities, all as imagined by an individual. Sweden is portrayed as a person with consciousness *and* collective and individual unconscious. It is intriguing that Annerstedt (1909) also makes reference to 'the soul of the Swedish people' in his speech:

> what makes Selma Lagerlöf's writings so lovable is that we always seem to hear in them an echo of the most peculiar, the strongest, and the best things that have ever moved the soul of the Swedish people. Few have comprehended the innermost nature of this people with a comparable love.
>
> (Annerstedt 1909)

The ideal of community as offering infinite continuity, despite the natural and inevitable occurrence of individual deaths, certainly resonates as a strong undercurrent within Lagerlöf's text.

Children also figure in the futurity suggested by an eco-critical reading of the book. Over and over again the child characters portrayed by Lagerlöf point the way forward to the adults that surround them. For example, there are the children who show their disbelieving parents that it is possible to reforest a bare fire-swept mountain (Lagerlöf 1930: 175–80). There is Osa, the goose-girl, who suffers through all manner of vicissitudes yet finds and restores the father that deserted the family, bringing him home to Skåne from Lapland. Even the parents of the protagonist, Nils, fare ill in his absence and have their fortunes restored when he returns and can show them how to cure the lame horse and keep their home and the live geese:

> But the boy still lingered at the threshold. He could not comprehend why they were so glad to see him – such as he was. Then his mother came and put her arms around him and drew him into the room, and he knew that he was all right.
>
> 'Mother and father!' he cried. 'I'm a big boy. I am a human being again!'
>
> (Lagerlöf 1930: 335)

This is a tale in which conscious and unconscious content seem harmonised. In the inner story the apparent 'shadow' of the natural aggression of male creatures and the trickster-boy can emerge, but are accommodated by the wise maternal, as all meet through the tiny 'child' sent by a mysterious spiritual father in a dream vision. Although, like the versions of the 'Tom Thumb' story encountered in Chapter 2, Tummetott's trickster aspect must be transcended by being put to positive use (as in action against Smirre Fox), the maternal sphere is neither devouring nor violently rejected. It is in the figure of Tummetott (a generic nomination used more frequently than the character's personal name, Nils) that all is drawn together, it is in 'his' story that the mythical pattern metaphorically associated with individuation is seen.

The outer story offers similar patterning, as nature and instinct are harmonised with 'man's' conscious efforts to survive in and preserve the land. The whole speaks to an absence of unresolved tension between 'real' and fantasy, between female and male, between inner and outer vision.

The Little Grey Men

If equilibrium is suggested by Lagerlöf's text, it is a marked absence from the books by 'BB' (particularly the second), which, in ecocritical terms, can be read as a tirade against anthropocentric forces that are seen as destructive to the land and to the natural creatures that inhabit it. At every level the books are darkly concerned with absence and death.

However, it may well be the lack of any sustained mention of the Second World War that is most noticeable to readers, given that *The Little Grey Men* was first published in 1942. In this first of the books by 'BB', war is not given any great degree of story space or portrayed as having any impact on the lives of the gnomes, or, indeed, on any of the other characters.

It is, however, tacitly acknowledged in the background, through the medium of a listing of the toys owned by a small boy, Robin Clobber, who possesses soldiers, tanks and aeroplanes and desires a working Spitfire or a gun for his birthday ('BB' 1978: 202). It is also tacitly acknowledged when the same boy refers to the war in adventure terms when he decides to pretend that the *Jeanie Deans* (his working model boat) is actually on convoy duty, carrying supplies to Britain and consequently under constant German attack ('BB' 1978:

205). But even the latter is effectively a plot device and focuses on the manner in which the tiny gnomes acquire transport after being shipwrecked on an inhospitable island in the midst of a lake on Robin's father's estate. Robin's game is significant only in that it causes him to load the boat with peppermint creams and other similar 'supplies' which the gnomes are more than glad to make use of. By implication the message seems to be that the war may feature in the world of the 'large' (an adult place) while in the 'little' world (where there is no room for adults) created by 'BB', it is relegated to the status of a 'game' in contrast with the 'real' business of life: survival in the natural wild.

Curiously, the war surfaces more significantly (though equally briefly), in the sense of impinging directly on the lives of the protagonists, in the second (post-war) text, *The Little Grey Men Go Down the Bright Stream* (1948):

> Strange lights hung in the sky at night, swinging balefully, like priests' censers. Curious rod-like beams sprang up and toyed with the stars, and sometimes red glares smouldered afar off, as of immense bonfires. Distant doors seemed to slam and the droning thunderbirds passed over invisible but menacing.
>
> ('BB' 1988: 159)

With talk of a 'thunderbird dropping its eggs' ('BB' 1988: 159), the reference is likely to have been clear to all readers at the time of first publication (readers who may well have recently experienced bombing at first hand); the war emerges here as a powerful backdrop to a story that despairs of an England in the grip of the destructive forces of technology. It is further emphasised when the gnomes' temporary home in a derelict mill collapses in what is clearly intended to be read as an air raid, given the surrounding references:

> Rumbling Mill suddenly heaved up and groaned aloud from every ancient timber and joist. Tiles crashed loudly to the ground and the old rose-red chimney, after tottering and swaying for a split second like a drunken man, plunged down with an appalling splash into the mill pool, shearing away the peak of the gable and driving a shoal of perch quite frantic with terror.
>
> This sudden shock was so terrifying, so outrageous, that for a moment or two everybody was frozen with fear.
>
> ('BB' 1988: 159)

Worlds begin to collide, as there is an adult incursion into the peace and tranquillity of the gnomes' existence and they are forced to flee across the Irish Sea to find a new and saner habitat.

Despite the brevity of the treatment of war, perhaps still regarded as much too painfully close at the time of writing to make comfortable matter for 'BB's' implied child readership, death and absence are still very much apparent. At surface story level there are dead companions; a missing brother; a murdered mortal; attempted fratricide; loss of home and habitat; danger of death – by drowning, by being hunted and eaten, and by burning. All this is very far away from the cosier worlds of fairies of the kind depicted in many twentieth-century stories for children, such as those created in picture form by Mabel Lucie Attwell, and the kind 'BB' condemns as 'ridiculous beings in tinsel frocks with gold stars in their hands and with gauzy wings sticking out of their backs, pictures which of course are very pretty but are not like fairies at all' ('BB' 1978: 171).

War is not the only comparative absence from the books: there is an absence (as noted previously) of conventional fairytale trappings; an absence of significant female characters (which I will discuss later) and of significant child characters. With regard to the latter, the human children that are depicted (very infrequently) as minor characters, with the exception of the fairly sympathetic account of landowner's son Robin Clobber, are generally 'nuisances,' such as the 'miller's brats' ('BB' 1978: 16), one of whom tries to hit the kingfisher with 'a stone from his catapult' ('BB' 1978: 16).

The world of the little grey men is, on the other hand, distinctly adult and distinctly male. 'BB's' gnomes are, in many superficial ways, similar to Tolkien's 'hobbit' character Bilbo Baggins,[27] though largely lacking in the humour and tricksterish aspects of Bilbo. They are depicted as elderly country gentlemen: they smoke pipes, drink wine, fish, and have both a code of manners of their own and a sense of existing within a natural hierarchical structure. They address the kingfisher bird as 'your Majesty' ('BB' 1978: 15) and the heron as 'Sir Herne' ('BB' 1978: 67), but, equally, they demand respect from and have a paternalistic view of most of the smaller animals they encounter.

It is difficult to suggest that the three little grey heroes of the first text, Dodder, Sneezewort and Baldmoney, are, in any sense, surrogate children within the text, although they are depicted as exhibiting behaviour that might be regarded as child*ish* with sibling squabbles, sulking and tears much in evidence: 'Dodder lay in the cave, sobbing violently. Nobody came near him, no one showed him sympathy. And because of this he was brought to his senses. Self-pity never helped anybody, least of all a gnome' ('BB' 1978: 58).

In the second book, however, a gnome character emerges who may be regarded as more of a child protagonist, and that is the 'odd-gnome-out' Cloudberry. Cloudberry is largely absent from the action of the first book, though providing the impetus for the remaining gnomes' initial adventures as his prolonged absence causes his brothers to set out along the banks of the Folly Brook to search for him. While Baldmoney, Sneezewort and Dodder search on land and on water, Cloudberry has been in the air (as readers learn at the end of the tale) having adventured north to Spitzbergen with the wild geese. He appears as much more of a carefree (and careless) adventurer and there is much of the irrepressible child in his appearances. However, in the second book, Cloudberry is actively portrayed as the villain of the piece. Continually put down by his brothers, particularly Dodder, as he attempts to tell all and sundry of his adventures, his 'tricksterish' activities become darker and darker and he finally makes an attempt on his brothers' lives. Throughout, the narrator controls readers' potential responses to this possible 'child' – guiding readers to note all that is reprehensible in his actions and hindering any potential for reader-identification with the character.

In fact, the gnome protagonists are all presented from a distanced observational viewpoint by an adult-sounding and omniscient storyteller/narrator, one who actually addresses an implied child narratee/reader directly from time to time. For example, in telling of the gnomes restricting their travels to the twilight hours, the narrator, claiming a link with childhood adds:

> Perhaps this accounts for the fact that our Great-Grandparents so seldom caught sight of the Little People, and even on those very rare occasions when they did, they put it down to some trick of the imagination. . . . Grown-up people, it is safe to say, hardly ever see them. Why? You will ask, quite naturally. And I should answer, it is because they have grown up.
>
> ('BB' 1978: 77–8)

Effectively, by the use of this device, child readers are likely to remain distanced from any sense of identification with the gnomes (though perhaps sympathising, empathically, with their plight) and encouraged instead to 'watch' their adventures from a safe viewpoint controlled by the voice of the narrator and implied author of the work.

The gnomes are further distanced by being described in terms that emphasise their age, two having wrinkly, grey-whiskered faces ('BB' 1978: 12–13), one lacking teeth (Sneezewort) and another with a wooden leg (Dodder). At one stage in the book the narrator tells readers that the youngest of the four gnomes, Sneezewort, 'was born long before Julius Caesar landed in Britain, but that is awfully young for a gnome' ('BB' 1978: 223). Yet, in their size and in the suggestion of such longevity as to be 'almost' immortality, there is some sense in which they do have the eternal child motif implicit in their creation.

The writer's account of their longevity and absence of memory of their earliest days creates another significant, implicit rather than explicit, absence, that of a mother. There is, overall, a lack of female characters of any note within these books. Those that do appear are generally presented as minor, silly and ineffectual, whether the unnamed wife of Spink the chaffinch, who, 'like all females the world over, loved a juicy bit of gossip' ('BB' 1978: 31) or Robin Clobber's mother, who causes Robin's birthday gift, the boat, to be lost: 'Robin began to run along the bank; Mummy too, was anxious – how silly of her to forget the rudder! Just like a woman!' ('BB' 1978: 206).

'BB's' mothers are stereotypes rather than archetypes, but perhaps the depiction of a masculine world that excludes and denies the female does, in some fashion, echo the English 'Tom Thumb' fairytale character. Where 'realist' story meets fairytale 'BB's' suppression and repression of female characters is echoed in the apparent absence of symbolic images of the archetypal mother and could well be regarded as comparable to the surfacing of shadow images of the same.

While individual mothers are absent or inadequate, the writer does focus, at all levels, on an all-powerful image of masculine fathering associated with nature and myths of Pan, here described by 'BB' in the conventional image of a masculinised and partially theriomorphic god of nature. The figure of Pan looms, in omnipotent fashion, over both books. In the first, the gnomes encounter a gamekeeper, known to the creatures of Crow Wood as the Giant Grum, who deals death, with his gun, to all but the pheasants he is employed to care for. Desiring to take revenge on the gamekeeper, following the man's shooting of a friendly otter, Dodder, the oldest of the gnomes, calls on the god Pan for help. In a solemn gathering of all the wild creatures of the wood, the 'Woodland God' appears, 'a wondrous Being, his cloven feet in a circle of glow-worm light' ('BB' 1978: 142–3).

Although the pheasants try to argue against the general outcry, maintaining that the man has planted the trees of this wood for their home and feeds and protects them, Pan is swift to pronounce the death sentence: ' "The woods were here before man walked the earth, though he can tame the trees and work his will upon them, even as he has tamed you, O pheasants" . . . "Your wish is granted, the Giant shall no longer walk Crow Wood" ' ('BB' 1978: 145). In quite a chilling scene, Pan causes the 'Giant Grum' to feel ill and lie down to sleep in the woods, together with his dog. While both are unconscious, Dodder crams six oak leaves, given to him by Pan, into the muzzle of the gun. When the man awakes, he sees in a nearby branch a 'tiny man in a batskin cap and coat' ('BB' 1978: 149). Taunted by the gnome and his companion grey squirrel, who both throw sticks and spit at him, the gamekeeper fires at them and the gun explodes, 'blowing him out like a light' ('BB' 1978: 150).

In a later, similar, demonstration of omnipotence and violent justice, Pan 'saves' Dodder, Baldmoney and Sneezewort from the murderous intentions of their brother Cloudberry. As discussed earlier, Cloudberry is alienated from the other three by his unwillingness to accept Dodder's assumption of leadership and the older gnome's constant belittling of what the narrator repeatedly refers to as Cloudberry's boastful account of his adventures. Ultimately Cloudberry plans to murder the other three (and their animal companions), by introducing poisonous toadstools to their mushroom supper, aiming to be the last gnome left in England:

> But Pan had willed it otherwise. It was Pan who whispered into the ear of the Worm of Death [a poisonous adder] away on Bantley Heath that three white owlets in down would make him a fine supper. It was Pan who guided those sinister coils to Rumbling Mill and it was he who cleverly arranged that the panic-stricken Cloudberry, his guilty mind full of his own dreadful project, should elect at that moment to come tumbling down the mill-house stairs!
>
> ('BB' 1988: 146–7)

For child readers who are guided by the narrator, the book suggests, at story level, that those who have a child-like accord with nature will ultimately be protected by the personal intervention of a masculine god-figure. The implied authorial message seems to be that although individuals may fail, or turn to evil, 'god' and his chosen followers will be there to protect. In accordance with this, Dodder, given added status by the portrayal of his relationship with Pan (the god even knows his name and addresses him as 'venerable Dodder': 'BB' 1978: 145), is depicted as enacting parenting, particularly where this draws attention to the failings of natural parents:

> And everywhere the fields, woods and copses were full of baby things just out of the nest . . .
>
> Dodder was able to save many a little life. He found a baby song thrush which had fallen into the river. He fished it out and sat it in the sun until it had dried and then gave the mother thrush a sound rating for neglecting her children.
>
> He found a young blackbird, whose parents had deserted it, a puffed-up ball of misery who was unable to find any food for itself. Dodder dug it worms from a mossy bank, taking care to kill the worm before giving it to the baby bird, just as he had seen the old birds do.
>
> ('BB' 1988: 151–2)

Here child readers entering the world of the text are guided by the writer-as-narrator, perhaps self-envisioned as 'wise old man', into an encounter with a secure, and possibly therefore attractive, natural hierarchical system in which all creatures, other than humankind, have their place. Any transgression is punishable by an implacably just, death-dealing yet protective, masculine mother/father figure, and 'his' appropriately worshipful followers as the surface adventure meshes with the arising of symbolic content in the apparent 'dress' of the mythological figure of Pan. However, in 'BB's' envisioning of a god-nominated Pan, there is little of the 'wild' nature god and much that speaks to a stern father god, as in the patriarchal figure of western Christianity.

The writer-as-narrator and Dodder may well be inwardly experienced by readers as aspects of the archetypal 'wise old man', under the aegis of this manifestation of a god 'self'. Significantly, Dodder's assumption of the position of mature leader of the group stems from the moment in which he succeeds in drawing Pan to Crow Wood, since, returning from his solitary vigil, readers are told: 'His face seemed transfigured, as though a great weight had been lifted from him: the other stood dumbfounded. This was a new Dodder and they felt embarrassed' ('BB' 1978: 140–1). There appears, however, to be no glimmer of 'other', no female maternal or anima in this all-male archetypal imagining.

There is, however, the faintest suggestion of the existence of some primeval force linking mothering with the female sex in 'BB's' texts. Whether this emerges from the writer's conscious or unconscious is impossible to say, but a telling mention of the sea as archetypal mother arises, as if unbidden, in 'The Folly Brook Song', as the poem closes: 'No sleeping, no slowing,/The sky in my face,/Eternally flowing,/I ripple, I race,/Impatient to rest/On the Grey Mother's breast' ('BB' 1978: 251). The Folly Brook itself is also created as a nurturing image, though never explicitly presented as a female presence. It provides many of the creatures in the book with home and food, and beyond this, a sense of loving security:

> Lulled by the Folly water, which sent back an echo from the dark tunnel of the trees, the gnomes soon fell fast asleep and the music of the stream was a comforting lullaby, one that was familiar, and which had always been part of all their sleeping and waking life. Even in this strange and somewhat sinister place it sang as sweetly as ever and soon the eventful night was quite forgotten in dreamless and untroubled slumber.
>
> ('BB' 1978: 95–6)

The account of the destruction of the Folly Brook, in the form that the creatures who live in and around it know, is quite as traumatic, if not more so, than the many deaths that occur during the course of the two books. Indeed, the chapter that describes this happening is titled 'The Death of the Folly' despite the fact that 'BB' asserts:

> But the Folly still lived. Even Man cannot kill a stream. That bright water, which burst from the earth and seemed its very life-blood, flowed still, though down another channel, a man-made channel of bolted iron, where no trees could grow and no voles or gnomes could live. Imprisoned it was, away from the sunlight and the open air. No longer could it reflect the pale blue skies of Spring, no longer would the swallows dip into it chattering joyously, but still it flowed, albeit asleep.
>
> ('BB' 1988: 39–40)

In this poignant description of the brook, particularly of its 'birth' and the notion of it flowing 'asleep', there is a sense of the fairytale child, a 'Sleeping Beauty', given life by the earth, but imprisoned in 'bolted iron' by Man.[28] The androgynous stream, which is continually reborn from the earth and journeys ceaselessly to the 'Grey Mother' until the moment of its incarceration in a man-made burial chamber (that has penetrated but is not *of* the earth), is a potent imagining of a Persephone figure. Here the writing, in speaking of the repression of the vitally living stream as it is driven underground, in a dark and nature-careless age, parallels the other repressions/absences/gaps that all speak, tellingly, to a mood of darkness and despair, pervading book and land. It is as if the image of mothering arises from a deeply unconscious part of the writer's creation, repressed at the story level, but arising in elemental imagery of a quasi-divine mother (sea) and abused child (stream) living under constant threat in a tale in which humankind is experienced as shadow.

It is here that the tensions between surface and depths are fully exposed. On the one hand, a patriarchal model of life is celebrated in the persons of the gnomes, wild creatures and, above all, Pan. On the other hand, mortal kind (and attendant technology) is the all-engulfing shadow, destroying everything in its path and leading to the need for the gnomes to flee England.

Even among the gnomes there is a sense of the possible emergence of shadow aspects that must be suppressed. Returning to the tale's relationship with the fairytale early trickster 'Tom Thumb', the shadow trickster, in Cloudberry's image, is crushed and voided by the god. The child motif, if an image of such can reside in the remaining gnomes, offers no prospect for futurity; they are dying out, the last of their kind. At a surface level, without females they cannot be renewed. At a deeper level, the subterranean stream speaks to an even greater sense of loss.

Unlike the situation as it relates to Nils' adventures in Lagerlöf's odyssey, in 'BB's' tale Cloudberry's trip with the wild geese is derided and his accounts suppressed. If archetypal strands emerge in this tale, they seem to offer a metaphorical enactment of patriarchal myth. There is no place for the trickster 'wild' child and adventurer, who must forfeit his life if he offers resistance to the rigid code of the senex (envisioned as Dodder); the wild nature god, Pan, is re-dressed in an image of the Christian God, though in this incarnation omnipotent only on a small scale. The 'shadow' is somehow all humankind, and a vengeful God erupts in 'BB's' account, but is impotent in halting humankind's downward spiral into darkness.

Chapter 5

Post-war Britain and Europe

In this chapter I shall continue to explore post-Second-World-War texts featuring individual miniature protagonists. Here I am focusing on case studies in which the miniature character is very much the child-hero of her or his tale. Again, I am seeking to discover what may be revealed of collective unconscious content, hidden within the creative imagining of the child motif in the metaphorical form of the miniature, and what the 'clothing' of such archetypal appearances may suggest with regard to the time-spirit of the age in which these stories were written and first published. Of particular interest here, however, is the extent to which the 'child' as hero appears, on the one hand, in alliance with other archetypal images (conjoined or partnered) and, on the other, disguised within a 'classic-realist' construction of a thinking/feeling child-person.

Arrietty

Mary Norton's series of books (1952 onwards) about the 'borrowers' follows the lives of a family of tiny hominiform characters – the Clocks, Homily, Pod, and their daughter Arrietty – who are said, initially, to live beneath the floorboards of an old country house. The house, owned by a bedridden old lady, Great Aunt Sophy, is presided over, in its Mistress's comparative absence, by Mrs Driver, the coldly callous housekeeper. It is the temporary home of a boy (never named), who has been sent to his Great Aunt's house, in order to recuperate from rheumatic fever, by parents who reside in India. The boy, readers are told, is 9 years of age, and Norton portrays him as lonely and in need of a loving family. The housekeeper, as substitute female care-giver, is an unsympathetic figure, of whom the boy says: 'She's fat and has a moustache and gives me my bath and hurts my bruise and my sore elbow and says she'll take a slipper to me one of these days' (Norton 1992a: 74).

The characters in the central part of the story are introduced to readers by a framing tale, in which an elderly lady, Mrs May, tells their story to a young girl, Kate. As with Lagerlöf's appearance in Nils' tale, Norton's words are intended to imply that she is the young girl, adding another layer of ambiguity for child readers, who are constantly teased with an 'are-they-aren't-they-real?' conundrum in the outer part of the borrowers' story:

> It was Mrs May who first told me about them. No, not me. How could it have been me – a wild, untidy, self-willed little girl who stared with angry eyes and was said to crunch her teeth? Kate, she should have been called. Yes, that was it – Kate. Not that the name matters much either way: she barely comes into the story.
>
> (Norton 1992a: 7)

If readers are intended to believe in an implied authorial presence – another 'writer-as-character' – Kate's prime significance is in 'her' position as narratee of the tale, which is then, in terms of origination, pushed backward two layers: first to Mrs May who tells the tale to Kate and then to the nameless boy, Mrs May's long-dead brother.

> 'He [Mrs May's little brother] was such a tease. He told us so many things – my sister and me – impossible things. . . . He wanted to impress us; he wanted, perhaps, to shock us. And yet' – she looked into the fire – 'there was something about him – perhaps because we were brought up in India among mystery and magic and legend – something that made us think that he saw things that other people could not see; sometimes we'd know he was teasing, but at other times – well, we were not so sure'.
>
> (Norton 1992a: 11)

The words on the page hint at an extra-textual existence for the story, locating the miniature creatures within it in a different chronotopical moment, in a context aligned with 'mystery and magic and legend', and claiming a succession of oral and, ultimately, literary storytellers handing on a 'real' tale of fantasy beings.

Arrietty, Norton's minute-female-child protagonist, is created in such a way that suggests an archetypal 'Thumbelina-type' image from fairytale, however, this symbolic part of the character is aligned with the sense of a 'real' thinking, feeling person, trapped in a tiny body in an endless existence of dust, darkness and fear of discovery:

> I don't think it's so clever [Arrietty cried] to live on alone, for ever and ever, in a great, big, half-empty house; under the floor, with no one to talk to, no one to play with, nothing to see but dust and passages, no light but candlelight and firelight and what comes through the cracks.
>
> (Norton 1992a: 48)

Her origins are not portrayed as being supernatural (though she is a fantasy creation), but both her solitariness and her 'at oneness' with the natural world are emphasised, as are the dangers she faces in her total vulnerability – and there *is* something miraculous simply in the idea of a tiny child living beneath the floorboards, albeit with such prosaic parents as Pod and Homily Clock. In fairytale form the 'child' could be suggestive of a metaphorical manifestation of the full-sized boy's anima, trapped in the depths of the house he inhabits, given that Norton suggests, repeatedly, that Arrietty is fiction within fiction, a creation of this lonely boy's imagination. Equally, the roles may be read as reversed in Norton's portrayal, with Arrietty cast as the storyteller's conjoined ego/hero of the text, adventuring into the unknown, facilitated by the power of Norton's, perhaps unconsciously stimulated, imaging of a symbolic encounter with overwhelming animus in the form of the boy. Once symbolic content is submerged beneath the surface of such complex characters, child readers identifying with their heroes may absorb a multiplicity of personal interpretations (both conscious and unconscious) of such fictional encounters. Even the adult 'borrowers' surrounding Arrietty are symbolically children, trapped in a newly-alien world.

As with the other post-war stories explored in this part of my book, there is a sense of drawing back from events of the writer's immediate past. Here Norton sets her story in a time period well before the Second World War (the first book of Norton's cycle is explicitly set in the past.) Poignantly, the full-sized 'boy' of the first book dies off-stage in another conflict, briefly lamented in the framing story of the first book of the series: 'He was killed . . . many years ago now, on the North-West Frontier. He became colonel of his regiment. He died what they call "a hero's death"' (Norton 1992a: 11).

Although the world wars of Norton's recent past are not overtly mentioned, her creation of Mrs Driver (a stereotypical villain in the surface story) is redolent with intimations of archetypal content as a conjoint image of shadow-mother. In an echo of the horrors of the real world, Norton's character tries to exterminate the tiny family by having them gassed, in the full knowledge (Norton advises) that they are not literally the 'vermin' Mrs Driver terms them, but minute scraps of human-like creatures. Norton does not flinch from acknowledging the darkness that may be found in the human psyche, despite the book's implied child audience.

At the end of the first book in the series, the 'borrower' family are forced to 'emigrate' (as Norton has them term it) from their home when Mrs Driver discovers their existence, because of the boy and his relationship with Arrietty, and calls in the rat-catcher. No matter how much the boy pleads and cries and promises to move the tiny family, Mrs Driver is not to be placated, pitilessly dragging the child to his room and gloating:

> 'They'll be moved all right,' she said. 'Don't worry. The rat-catcher will know how. . . . Once you've found the nest,' she went on, dropping her voice to a vicious whisper as they passed Aunt Sophy's door, 'the rest is easy!'
>
> (Norton 1992a: 139)

In this exchange, the bipolar relationships between the tiny borrowers and the 'giant' human creatures that are, so easily, able to threaten and engulf their world, are clearly presented. On the one hand, there is the powerful and destructive adult-female; on the other, there is the vulnerable, but loving, male child. Both can, on a whim, snuff out the borrower family's existence.

Though later drawn into a loving relationship with Arrietty, the boy, too, is presented as fearing and threatening her in their first meeting:

> 'Don't move!' said a voice, and the voice, like the eye, was enormous but, somehow hushed – and hoarse like a surge of wind through the grating on a stormy night in March. . . .
>
> There was a pause and Arrietty, her heart pounding in her ears, heard the breath again, drawn swiftly into the vast lungs.

> 'Or,' said the voice, whispering still, 'I shall hit you with my ash stick.'
>
> Suddenly Arrietty became calm. 'Why?' she asked. How strange her own voice sounded! Crystal thin and harebell clear, it tinkled on the air.
>
> 'In case,' came the surprised whisper at last, 'you ran towards me, quickly through the grass . . . in case,' it went on, trembling a little, 'you scrabbled at me with your nasty little hands.'
>
> (Norton 1992a: 66)

The shadow is imaged in human form and is portrayed as far more of a threat to the survival of Arrietty than natural predators in the wild. When the borrowers are depicted escaping from Mrs Driver and fleeing to the copses and fields, narratee Kate fears that they cannot survive with predators such as weasels, crows and stoats all around: '"Yes," agreed Mrs. May, "of course there was danger. There's danger everywhere, but no more for them than for many of us. At least they didn't have *wars*"' (Norton 1992a: 154).

Arrietty's journey through the narrative is indeed one fraught with danger. She makes friends with full-sized human boys; bravely faces death in the form of attempted gassing by the rat-catcher (in *The Borrowers*), at the predatory claws and teeth of Mild Eye's cat (in *The Borrowers Afield*), and those of Tom Goodenough's escaped ferret (in *The Borrowers Afloat*) and the prospect of freezing or starving to death in the natural world as winter sets in. Twice she is threatened with capture and a life of imprisonment as an object of curiosity in a 'freak' show, once in a Gipsy's bird-cage and then in the ultimate horror of a glass-fronted house. She is portrayed as fearing such fates more than death itself. Her father tries to protect her from the first '"Quiet," breathed Pod, "better the cage than the ferret." "No," thought Arrietty, "better the ferret"' (Norton 1992b: 166). But Pod, too, understands the full horror of living out his life in such a prison when confronted with the prospect of the house in which Mr and Mrs Platter intend to keep them, described, so chillingly, in *The Borrowers Aloft*:

> One side of their cage-house, they [Arrietty, Homily and Pod] learned, was to be made of thick plate-glass, exposing their home life to view. 'Good and heavy' the glass would have to be – Mr Platter had insisted, describing the 'layout' to Mrs Platter – nothing the borrowers could break; and fixed in a slot

> so the Platters could raise it for cleaning. The furniture was to be fixed to the floor and set in such a way that there should be nothing behind which they might hide.
>
> (Norton 1993b: 81)

Without the distancing of fantasy miniature forms, these are horrifying episodes for a child to experience vicariously, yet the adventure format of the surface story offers the consolation of likely positive endings and the dangers are relative to the character's size, possibly giving child readers something of a superior vantage point. Yet this is dependent upon the level of feeling of identification with the hero that may be experienced by individual readers. Joseph Appleyard (1994), drawing, to some extent, on Margaret Meek, suggests that reading:

> focuses on issues of identity, in the image of the powerful or clever hero or heroine who in one disguise or another is the principal archetype [not, here, used in a fully Jungian sense] of the stories most school-age children read. The prominence of this archetype suggests that a main reward of reading fictional stories at this age is to satisfy the need to imagine oneself as the central figure who by competence and initiative can solve the problems of a disordered world.
>
> (Appleyard 1994: 59)

Concentrating on the first two books in the series, it is interesting to discover to what extent glimmers of the archetypal alliances found lurking in the 'Tömmelise' story surface in Arrietty's tale. Although Andersen created his tiny maiden overtly as a heroine for children, the fairytale format, together with Andersen's eye to an adult audience, renders her into symbolic form, as discussed in Chapter 3, of relevance to both sides of the adult–child equation. Kangkang's use of her is, similarly, overtly symbolic: in these appearances, the imaginal form of the symbolic divine child/anima or child/Kore alliance is not hidden within a liaison with a 'classic realist' form of character creation. Mary Norton's character, Arrietty, however, is a complex meld including the adult writer's simulation of a thinking, feeling child and adolescent. Throughout the 'borrowers' series of books – *The Borrowers* (1952), *The Borrowers Afield* (1955), *The Borrowers Afloat* (1959), *The Borrowers Aloft* (1961) and *The Borrowers Avenged* (1982) – readers are given access to the tiny girl's thoughts and dreams, so that the symbolic, archetypal content metaphorically expressed in the size of the character is frequently obscured by the semblance of a 'real' child with whom child readers might well identify.

Both Andersen's and Norton's protagonists are distanced, at least initially, by a 'framing' story, which serves to make these tiny girl-children creatures of fairytale and possibly of dream or imagination. In Andersen's tale, he assumes the position of storyteller/narrator and credits the Swallow with making Tömmelise's story available to him. In Norton's tale, there are fictions within fictions within fictions. As mentioned earlier, the narrator recounts a story told to her as a child (naming her childhood self Kate, but encouraging readers to believe it is indeed the current storyteller) by an elderly lady, Mrs May, who attributes it in turn to her brother, the 'boy' of the inner story. It is even hinted that the boy may have invented the story to impress his sisters, for Mrs May, though crediting the account to a written version in Arrietty's Memoranda book, teasingly undermines this:

> 'Then that [the account in Arrietty's book] proves it,' she [Kate] said finally, . . .
>
> 'Not quite,' said Mrs. May.
>
> 'Why not?' asked Kate.
>
> 'Arrietty used to make her "e's" like little half-moons with a stroke in the middle–'
>
> 'Well?' said Kate.
>
> Mrs. May laughed and took up her work again. 'My brother did too,' she said.
>
> (Norton 1992a: 159)

So Arrietty, in a fiction within a fiction, is presented as the possible dream child of a male ego (though brought to life, in this instance, through the pen of an adult-female writer).

Traces discernible in the fairytale that clearly arise in the literary text are elements of the Demeter-Persephone myth, with its metaphorical subtext of underlying patterns, perhaps from the collective unconscious, of maturation, emergent sexuality and the liminality of such states. Arrietty's struggle, though a reversal in that she is born beneath the floorboards and fights to emerge from this underground existence, still offers a contrasting underground/overground world. There are implicit parallels between the fairytale, drawing upon mythic content, and Norton's book – for both Thumbelina and Arrietty are portrayed as revelling in nature and in daylight. Both are maidens in harmony with the surface world of light. As she is about to marry the mole Inchelina (Thumbelina) laments: '"Farewell . . . Farewell, you beautiful sun!" Inchelina lifted her hands up toward the sky. ... She saw a little red flower. Embracing it, she said: "Farewell! And give my love to the Swallow if you ever see him"' (Andersen 1994: 36). In similar fashion, Arrietty rails against an underground life and later enjoys the freedom of an outside world, with the narrator expressing the character's inner delight at her first steps outside: 'Oh, glory! Oh, joy! Oh, freedom! The sunlight, the grasses, the soft, moving air and half-way up the bank, where it curved round the corner, a flowering cherry-tree!' (Norton 1992a: 63).

However, Norton's character seeks more than just daylight and freedom from a dark, lonely and dreary material existence; as hero of her tale, Arrietty seeks to grow and become independent – to learn about the world, as in her shared afternoons with the lonely human boy when he turns the pages of the books he brings and Arrietty, leaning against his ear, reads to him, discovering that: 'this earth on which they lived turning about in space did not revolve, as she had believed, for the sake of little people. "Nor for big people either," she reminded the boy when she saw his secret smile' (Norton 1992a: 119).

Thumbelina (spoken of by Andersen's narrator as loving, gentle and kind, but never described as an independence seeker) is saved, in turn, by a Swallow whose life *she* has saved and is taken to a suitably tiny bridegroom, in a suitably ethereal place to settle down. Arrietty, though contemplating marriage with Spiller, the only young male borrower she has met by the end of Norton's third book in the series, *The Borrowers Aloft*, still thinks of this in terms of freedom and personal choice: '"He likes the out-of-doors, you see," said Arrietty, "and I like it, too"' (Norton 1993a: 121). She does not imagine that being married will prevent her from having her own life as an independent borrower, as a storyteller, as a writer. She is intent on escaping from the 'prison' of an underground existence, but not from the curtailment of freedom that marriage might bring.

Unlike her parents, Homily and Pod, and Andersen's nineteenth-century Thumbelina, in Norton's portrayal Arrietty revels in moving about on her own and effecting her own rescues: for example, overcoming her initial fear of the gigantic (to her) boy, despite his threats.

In a later book, when the family have been captured and imprisoned by Mr and Mrs Platter (greedy and callous human characters) Pod sinks into a deep depression and listlessly gives up all hope of escape until Arrietty – portrayed as untrammelled thinker and voracious reader – discovers the means by which the family are ultimately able to free themselves from the Platters' attic. Arrietty, inspired by a newspaper article on hot air ballooning (Arrietty is the only one in her family who can read), sees the possibility of making a borrower-sized flying machine out of a child's balloon attached to an empty strawberry punnet.

So Norton's Arrietty, unlike her fairytale counterpart, and despite still being willing to embrace some of her parents' values and learn from some of their experiences, is shown to be capable of moving on and to be unafraid of making her own path into a future which she has, in no small measure, helped to shape.

Within the text Norton explicitly acknowledges the intertextual connections readers may make between Arrietty and other 'little' peoples of times past. Readers of Norton's books are told, very firmly, that Arrietty is most certainly *not* a fairy. There is, however, some ambivalence regarding whether she believes in them. On the one hand, when the boy asks her if she can fly, a surprised Arrietty, answering 'no', asks him if he can: 'His face became even redder. "Of course not," he said angrily; "I'm not a fairy!" "Well, nor am I," said Arrietty, "nor is anybody. I don't believe in them"' (Norton 1992a: 69). Yet in the second book of the series, Norton describes how Arrietty would sometimes dress up in

> a skirt of violet leaves, stalks uppermost, secured about the waist with a twist of faded columbine, and, aping the fairies, a fox-glove bell for a hat. This, Arrietty thought as she stared at her bright reflection in the stagnant water of a hoof crater, might look all right on gnomes, elves, brownies, pixies, and what not, but she had to admit that it looked pretty silly on a common or garden borrower: for one thing, if the lip fitted the circumference of her head, the whole thing stood up too high like some kind of pinkish sausage or a very drawn-out chef's cap. Yet if, on the other hand, the lip of the bell flowed out generously in a gentle, more hat-like curve, the whole contraption slid down past her face to rest on her shoulders in a Ku-Klux-Klan effect.
>
> And to get hold of these bells at all was not easy: fox-glove plants were high. . . . Fairies did everything so gracefully:

> Arrietty, poor girl, had to hook down the plant with a forked stick and sit on it as heavily as she could while she plucked any bells within reach.
>
> (Norton 1992b: 134–5)

She is also only very loosely connected with the folktale character Tom Thumb, only, in fact, via the name as appropriated to the miniature (to human hands) books in her library. The list of Victorian miniature books given by Norton includes volumes which actually exist: for example one that is mentioned, Bryce's *Tom Thumb Dictionary*, was printed in the 1890s. Norton also, intriguingly, mentions the actual historical figure of 'General Tom Thumb':

> Arrietty's favourite [was] Bryce's *Tom Thumb Diary and Proverb Book*, with a saying for each day of the year and, as a preface, the life story of a little man called General Tom Thumb, who married a girl called Mercy Lavinia Bump. There was an engraving of their carriage and pair, with little horses – the size of mice. Arrietty was not a stupid girl. She knew that horses could not be as small as mice, but she did not realise that Tom Thumb, nearly two feet high, would seem a giant to a Borrower.
>
> (Norton 1992a: 19)

So, Norton, very pointedly, focuses on a living 'Tom Thumb' and ignores the tiny trickster of stories such as Richard Johnson's *The History of Tom Thumbe . . .* (see earlier discussion on pp. 33–40). Similarly, only the briefest of mentions is made of Swift's Lilliputians, as Miss Menzies (a human character in *The Borrowers Aloft* and *The Borrowers Avenged*) moves with 'great Gulliver-like strides over walls and railway lines, streets and alleyways' (Norton 1993b: 56) in the model village of Little Fordham, where the borrower family briefly live. More significantly, perhaps, there is no explicit mention of Thumbelina, despite the obvious parallels which give Andersen's creation the best claim to be a prototype for Arrietty Clock.

By conjoining the metaphorical child with the hero role and the simulated psyche of a 'real' child, Norton creates a complex formation for readers to relate with. As a creature of the 'conscious' text, Arrietty exemplifies the adolescent in that liminal stage of growing away from family and gaining confidence in her own, separate and individual life, as this extract from *The Borrowers Afield* demonstrates:

> Up and up she went. She found an old bird's-nest, the moss inside was straw-dry. She climbed into it and lay for a while and, leaning over the edge, dropped crumbled pieces of dried moss through the tangled branches below her; to watch them plummet between the boughs gave her, she found, an increased sense of height, a delicious giddiness which, safely in the nest she enjoyed. But having felt this safety made climbing out and on and up seem far more dangerous. 'Suppose I fell,' thought Arrietty, 'as those bits of moss fell, skimming down through the shadowy hollows and banging and bouncing as they go?' But as her hands closed round the friendly twigs and her toes spread a little to grip the bark, she was suddenly aware of her absolute safety – the ability (which for so long had been hidden deeply inside her) to climb.
>
> (Norton 1992b: 54)

But this passage is also redolent of images of rebirth and, indeed, Norton creates an implicit connection between her character and the natural world, using a link with the expression 'flying the nest' to establish in readers' minds the sense that Arrietty's burgeoning independence is an inevitable and natural part of the growth process. This link operates both at the level of 'classic realist' character maturing and at a deeper level in creating a metaphorical image of nature as the positive and ultimate mother/father, with their wild daughter reborn, in possession of her natural heritage, as a pivotal point for encounters between male and female, tiny and large, good and shadow. Yet the metaphor implicit in an image of Persephone also suggests that the character's independence is a compromise. The borrowers must always eventually find indoor security, albeit not beneath the floorboards of an old house. For part of the time the female-child hero must 'live in secret darkness' (Norton 1992b: 53); for part of the time the freedom of sunlight and air is hers: 'It was a glorious day, sunlit and rain-washed – the earth breathing out its scents. "This," Arrietty thought, "is what I have longed for; what I have imagined; what I knew existed – what I knew we'd have!"' (Norton 1992b: 51).

In terms of individuation, if this is an archetypal pattern that may speak to readers at some deep level from the underlying psychodynamic processes of the fairytale content of the text, Arrietty, as imaginal realisation of archetypal divine child, points the way to a future in which 'otherness' is resolved. She is the pivotal point through which large and small are able to encounter each other and ultimately, in some measure, cooperatively occupy the same spaces. Through her relationships with human beings, in story terms, Arrietty shows Norton's belief that the tiny can coexist with the large without being overwhelmed, though such encounters are fraught with danger and expressly forbidden by the character's parents. Perhaps, significantly, Arrietty is shown to be wiser and more independent than the human boys she effectively 'tames' and 'mothers'. As tropically-presented adult forms, the 'good' humans she encounters are drawn to and entranced by her presence. In speaking to and of her age, Norton, in her enduring books, seems to see hope and strength in images of the tiny and, at their worst, an horrific capacity for cruelty and abuse of power in shadowy adult figures, such as the housekeeper who cannot wait to have dead, gassed, borrowers 'laid out in sizes, on a clean piece of newspaper' (Norton 1992a: 145), such as the gipsy who would capture and sell them, and the Platters who would profit from their perpetual display. Andersen provides his passive female-child and maiden with a swallow-knight and an ethereal bridegroom – Norton's half 'real' half fantasy child carves her own way through danger and into the uncertainty of an unpredictable future above the floorboards.

Effectively there seems to be an equilibrium between the 'classic realist' female hero of the surface story, who points female child readers to their possible futures as independent human beings in a difficult world, and the underlying patterns, perhaps subconsciously imbibed, that help to 'dress' the archetypal content expressed as tiny maiden. Here 'she' survives encounters with the murderous and acquisitive envisioning of shadow and 'tames' the overwhelming animus of the giant (to her) boys 'she' encounters. The whole seems, metaphorically, to suggest a pattern of psychological maturation in a drawing together of multiple images of animus and nature (the latter as the ultimate mother/father figure) under her dominion.

However, there are potential tensions. Beyond nature as mother/father, there is no wise elder imagined within the text. If size and status is a metaphor for power, the powerful female figure is that of Mrs Driver, there is no comparable positive adult female until much later in the series (Miss Menzies in *The Borrowers Aloft* (1961) and *The Borrowers Avenged* (1982)).

Similarly, decentring Arrietty and interpreting the (dead) 'storyteller' as 'hero' of the tale, with Arrietty as powerful image of anima, despite her apparent vulnerability, creates a pattern in which there is no guiding transcendent male figure in the psychodynamic processes of the text, and the outer conscious world requires the masculine subject to live out the hero role to the death, while the female hero 'owns' the peace.

Maxie Pichelsteiner

Erich Kästner's *The Little Man* (first published as *Der Kleine Mann* in 1963) is the male, mainland-European counterpart of tiny Arrietty. German-born Kästner, whose books for adults were banned and publicly burnt by the Nazis, created the 'infinitely tiny' (Kästner 1975: 8) Maxie Pichelsteiner and his foster father, Professor Hokus von Pocus, with much tongue-in-cheek, humorous detail. Satirising greed, jealousy, acquisitiveness and the 'value' of fame, Kästner, nevertheless, through narratorial accounts of the minute boy's thoughts and dreams, builds up a sense of the vulnerability yet paradoxical strength of the child and of the loving relationship that develops between the Professor and his young charge.

As with Arrietty's tale, overt mention of specific outer-world conflicts is avoided, but death and danger is omnipresent. However, Kästner uses a narrator-controlled, darkly-comic account of such events as a brittle distancing device, so that when, for example, Maxie becomes an orphan, the account of his parents' deaths is given in the following fashion:

> When Maxie was six years old, he lost his parents. It happened in Paris, quite suddenly and unexpectedly. The couple had taken the lift up the Eiffel Tower in order to admire the beautiful view. But no sooner had they reached the topmost platform than a great gale sprang up, blew them off their feet and in a twinkling swept them up into space. . . . it was all over with Wu Fu and Chin Chin [the couple's circus stage names.] They were last seen, hand in hand, spinning away into the distance. Then they disappeared over the horizon.
>
> (Kästner 1975: 9)

This does not prevent a sense of poignancy creeping through, and it is here that Kästner's creation moves from joke-like baby, so small the doctor had to examine him through a magnifying glass to know he was male, to a child with all the sensibilities of a living, breathing human boy: 'the loss was saddest for Maxie who had loved his parents very, very much. He shed many a tiny tear into his tiny handkerchiefs. [. . . and] was so overcome with grief he felt he wanted to die too (Kästner 1975: 9).

A sense of the growing loving relationship between the full-size Professor and his tiny charge is expressively present, yet the deft touches of humour prevent the portrait of the two from sinking into mawkish sentimentality:

> At the end of his solemn address, the Professor said: 'The two little colleagues we are gathered here to mourn today left their Maxie in our charge. Shortly before their ill-fated ascent of the Eiffel Tower they brought him to my hotel room and asked me to keep an eye on him until they came back. And so I must keep an eye on him as long as I live, and shall do so gladly, with all my heart. Is that all right with you my boy?' Maxie who was peeping out of the breast pocket of the magician's professional tail-coat, sobbed: 'Oh yes, Hokus! It's all right with me.'
>
> (Kästner 1975: 10–11)

Throughout the narrative there is an intriguing tension between the intertextual antecedents that explicitly relate Kästner's creation to the archetypal imaginings of fairytale and Kästner's envisioning of the character as 'real' despite his fantastical size. Maxie relates implicitly to the fairytale 'Tom Thumb' in his abnormal minuteness, but although he enacts the 'tiny trickster' in his circus performance, all else about him partakes of the 'greatness' aspect of divine child, the potential unifying 'self' (in the manner of Arrietty as pivotal character in Norton's account). In his portrayal of a realistic child, while still drawing careful attention to Maxie's fairytale dimension, Kästner explicitly points to his character's resistance to 'tiny' roles:

> And Maxie would bury himself in one of his favourite books – *Hop o' My Thumb, Nils Holgersson, Memoirs of a Midget* or best of all, *Gulliver's Travels*. . . . But finally he would switch the light off, fall asleep and dream of Gulliver in Lilliput Land, where the inhabitants looked upon him as a giant.
>
> And this giant who strode over city walls and scuttled the enemy war-fleet was, naturally, no other than Maxie Pichelsteiner.
>
> (Kästner 1975: 17)

Maxie, as fictional reader-in-the-book, is always 'self-identified' as the hero, regardless of whether the protagonist in his 'favourite' book matches his 'real' 'Lilliputian' size ('[f]or even at the age of ten or twelve he only measured two inches precisely': Kästner 1975: 13). It is fascinating that Kästner's list of book titles relates to books that find their way into children's reading because they feature tiny characters. In his juxtaposition of fairytale, children's book and satire written for adult readers, Kästner exposes differences in the subject position offered to child readers between texts that situate the protagonist in the 'tiny' role – inviting reader identification – and those in which the reader is invited to take up a superior position to the tiny people, which are then 'objects' for the reader's gaze.

The relationship that Kästner portrays growing between tiny boy and the Professor exists simultaneously in 'realist' form, as exemplar of the loving small boy and surrogate father bond, and in metaphorical form, as expression of 'relatedness', here envisioned in the relationship between archetypal eternal child and wise old man. Within the incidents Kästner uses to create a sense of his protagonist's life history, two stand out as being particularly significant in terms of the relationship between boy and man. The first of these is a slightly bizarre dream sequence associated with Maxie at a moment when he has withdrawn, unnoticed, to leave the Professor and the lovely Rosa Marzipan the 'space' to become engaged.

Within the dream, Kästner portrays his protagonist as being separated from those who love him and in terror of being overwhelmed and crushed by the surrounding large-scale world. He climbs to safety on the shoulders of an elderly woman, who desires to take him home and 'mother' him:

> I think I can see you now. My dear young man, how tiny you are! A body doesn't see the likes of you every day. Won't you come home with me? Are you hungry? Are you tired? Have you a tummy-ache? Would you like me to put you to bed with a hot-water bottle?
>
> (Kästner 1975: 80)

All this is very redolent of the wish expressed by the full-size elderly parents of Tom Thumb for a child, 'be hee no bigger then my very Thumbe' (Opie and Opie 1974: 33) and of the elderly woman who desires to buy 'a tiny little child' (Andersen 1994: 29) of her own in Andersen's story. As a mother figure from Kästner's imagination, she is the antithesis of the youthful Rosa Marzipan and also of the Professor, who thus far in the text has been portrayed as enacting a form of male mothering that is protective, but not 'smothering'.

Going further into the dream world, Kästner's protagonist encounters the sinister and bearded 'PROFESSOR WACHSMUTH/ Doctor of medicine/Specialist in chronic discontent' (Kästner 1975: 80), very much the shadow of Maxie's beloved Professor Hokus von Pokus. Dr Wachsmuth could well be read as Kästner's caricature of Sigmund Freud; the whole dream sequence seems to echo Freudian ideas of dreams as 'wish-fulfilment' in that minute Maxie is depicted dreaming of becoming 'the same size as any normal boy of my age. No bigger, no smaller, no fatter, no thinner, and no freak like a rare stamp or a camel with three humps and no cheekier and not more timid and no more clever' (Kästner 1975: 85). Other intertextual references link the sequence with another (perhaps) dream sequence, the fantasy of Lewis Carroll's *Alice's Adventures in Wonderland*, as Maxie, like Alice down the rabbit hole, takes spoons of 'medicine' that make him first a giant and then reduce him to the size of a normal boy. The sequence ends with Maxie's tears, as within the dream Professor Hokus fails to recognise the new Maxie, who appears to have been supplanted by another tiny boy. Outside the dream, however, all is well:

> Maxie opened his eyes. Tears were still trickling between his eyelids. But he could see Hokus's concerned face bent above him. He smelt the scent of lily of the valley and realised that he was sitting in the flower-pot. On the balcony of his hotel room [*sic*]. He had only been dreaming, and all was well again.
>
> (Kästner 1975: 95)

Here a tiny fairytale protagonist dreams he is a 'real' boy, but is grateful to be tiny again if achieving full size means losing his loving guardian. Unlike Issun-boshi and Tom Thumb, if the Little Man is Kästner's imagining of the divine child motif, he appears here to be indissolubly bonded in a metaphorical link – male child/male father-mother – with the imaginal form of the wise elder.

In the other episode linked with a threat to the Little Man/ Professor bond Maxie is chloroformed and kidnapped. Kästner's narrator reveals that the hero is to be delivered by the villains, Otto and Bernard, to the impregnable South American stronghold of the sinister collector, Señor Lopez. Once there, he is to perform at the collector's whim for the rest of his life. In the story, manikin and wise Professor yearn to be reunited, but it is only the miniature child and hero that can bring this about by escaping from these shadow adult-male forms. Significantly, Kästner's caring adult character must wait and hope. Symbolically, the metaphorical child points the way to the future, as it is he who is the only one who can bring about the desired ending, something that is recognised by Rosa Marzipan:

> Rosa Marzipan shook her locks. 'There's only one person who can help us in this.'
>
> The manager opened his eyes wide. 'Who's that?'
>
> 'You're quite right,' Hokus told Rosa. 'He's our only hope.'
>
> 'But *who*?' repeated the manager.
>
> Miss Marzipan said simply: 'Maxie himself!'
>
> (Kästner 1975: 129)

Joining the group, in fairytale terms, Rosa is Kästner's creation of princess and fairy godmother rolled into one – as her name implies, she is sweetness personified, the female figure who is always 'deliciously' tempting, yet loving and irresistible to the Professor and to Maxie. There are few female figures in Kästner's text: Frau Holzer of Maxie's dream is an anxious elderly woman; the mother of the boy Jakob, who assists Maxie in his escape, leaves her son alone while she visits her sister and new baby and nags him (so much so that Jakob whispers to his father: 'Your spouse is unfortunately poisoning the one day of glory of your son who has recently come into a lot of money. Do you consider this proper or improper?': Kästner 1975: 172). It is Rosa Marzipan who demands to be read as Kästner's imaginal anima, adored in equal measure by his tiny protagonist and by the Professor (perhaps Kästner's alter-ego within the text). Although, in theory, the storyline places Rosa as surrogate mother (to be married to the caring Professor), the Professor is portrayed as filling both mothering and fathering roles in relation to the tiny child, and, beyond this, Kästner makes it plain that his character, though portrayed as child, is not immune to the erotic aspects of Miss Marzipan, as these exchanges between Rosa and Maxie show:

> 'What desperate-sounding names!' cried Rosa [hearing of the villains Otto and Bernard]. 'They give me goose-flesh all over.'

Maxie rubbed his hands. 'Show me! Marzipan with goose-flesh all over is something I'd very much like to see, just once.'

. . .

He [Maxie] was sitting on the table and allowing Rosa to feed him with bits of pineapple tart.

'Another little morsel?' she asked.

He shook his head. 'No thank you. All I want now is a little marzipan with goose-flesh.'

She wagged the cake-fork at him. 'That's not for little boys.'

'Oh, I know,' he teased. 'You're keeping it all for Hokus.'

Then Rosa blushed.

(Kästner 1975: 165–7)

However, the relationship is portrayed in a manner akin to that of Tom Thumb and the Fairy Queen – the Queen who kisses the tiny child is very much a similar imaginative form to Rosa, who holds 'The Little Man firmly in both hands and press[. . . es] his face gently against her marzipan cheek' (Kästner 1975: 164).

Kästner's simulated 'real' child in Maxie loves the Professor and Rosa, helping to bring them together. The fairytale child in the character is again the pivotal point, symbolically joining anima and wise elder. The shadow male figures are overcome, the shadow female figures are dismissed as stupid and irrelevant, Maxie crowns the trinity of anima, wise elder and himself or him-'self'.

At some level, whether consciously or unconsciously, both Norton and Kästner have joined fairytale elements with a realistically created world, as they reimagine collective archetypes and 'dress' them in the clothes of a European post-war world. There is a sense of futurity in their work and a mood of optimism in the willingness of the young protagonists to go forward into the unknown and lead the way for their elders. Yet here, as in 'BB's' text, there is a significant absence of any 'positive' 'wise elder' female figures – though perhaps Rosa represents hope for the future. It seems that mothering is the province of the young female or eternal nature, and can be added to the role of the wise male at will; there is no wise old woman – all traces of matriarchal succession are repressed.

Chapter 6

Suffering children

Moving away from examining individual miniature characters, in this chapter I shall be looking at appearances of 'races' of miniature people. The books I have chosen to explore, in common with my earlier case studies, were also first published during the post-war and 'Cold War' eras. The first of these is an English novel, T. H. White's (1947) *Mistress Masham's Repose*, and the second, which originated in Japan, Satoru Sato's (1959) *Daremo shiranai chiisa na kuni* (published in English in 1988 as *A Little Country No One Knows*). Given their origins, it will be interesting to see whether these texts show similar patterns to those envisioned in the early Tom Thumb and Issun-boshi fairytales explored in Part I, or whether they emerge in new variant 'dress'.

Lilliputians and Korobokkuru

As with the books by 'BB', Norton and Kästner, a significant feature of these two texts is located in absence, with minimal mention of the Second World War. In Satoru Sato's book, the horrors of warfare are acknowledged but, poignantly, condensed into three brief paragraphs – less than one page in a book of nearly two hundred:

> Then Japan went to war. Life grew steadily grimmer, leaving no room for dreams and memories. The fighting grew worse, and my father left home for the war. He went down with his ship in the South Seas about the time the bombing of Japan started.
>
> Our town was burned down. Only people's eyes seemed left alive. When I was still just a skinny kid in my last year of middle school, I was sent to work in a factory. And it was while I

> worked away, getting covered with grease, that my school burned down, too.
>
> Each day brought only pain, yet in a way it was also thrilling. We kids told one another about our houses' being burned down as if it was an exciting event. And the ultimate excitement was to be pursued and shot at by fighter planes – a deadly game of tag in which many of my less fortunate friends had already been caught. It makes me shudder to think of it now.
>
> But then the war ended.
>
> (Sato 1988: 38–9)

In White's text there is mention of playing at being 'General Eisenhower' (White 1972: 69) and 'tommy guns' (White 1972: 168), but the war that is covered explicitly lives between the pages of White's fiction in his Lilliputian schoolmaster's account of that between Lilliput and Blefescu – a terrible, but distanced, account of a war in which

> [c]orn Fields were burn'd, Cattle were driven away or slaughter'd, the Cities were subjected to a Number of Sieges which reduced the Inhabitants to Starvation, and the Emperors of both Realms died by each other's Hands, in single Combat outside the Walls of Mendendo. The Anarchy which subsequently prevail'd among the Leaders of the rival Factions, each of whom sought to draw the Power of Direction into his own Controul, reduced the Hopes of Reconciliation still further; and it was therefore upon a Civilization already tottering from its Foundations, Ma'am, that Captain John Biddel descended, after a Lapse of seventeen Moons, all of which had been devoted to Rapine and Destruction.
>
> (White 1972: 48)

Perhaps not surprisingly the books are, in some senses, nostalgic, in that they turn away from twentieth-century urban living. In White's text a third-person omniscient narrator looks toward the restoration of ancient estates and of the rightful heir (significantly, however, the heir is a child, and frequent irony, expressed through this very overt, and controlling narrator, undercuts any stable dependence on this as implied authorial view – particularly when taken alongside the overall critique of adults' abilities to act responsibly and with wisdom). Sato's little people, the Korobokkuru, fight to prevent the sacrifice of their natural environment to technological development, saving the hill that is their home from being bulldozed to make way for a highway.

The most striking similarity between the two texts is the way in which, perhaps unsurprisingly, the portrayals of such fairytale communities of minute manikins emphasise the vulnerability and the 'victim' status of White's and Sato's recreations of 'little' people. The writers' words give form to metaphorical envisionings of the child motif.

White's tiny characters live in a state of constant danger due to their relative size:

> the people lived a dangerous life. . . . For instance, there had been a family of magpies some thirty moons before, who had taken a fancy to young Lilliputians, and had carried of a dozen babies before they had been mastered. . . . Another danger was owls, worse than the danger of magpies. . . . instead of merely pouncing like the crow tribe, they came down vertically like dive-bombers, and it was impossible to slay them. There was no time. . . . As for the mainland trappers, their lives were in their hands. A fox was about as big as the National Gallery to them, and, as it could easily pounce across Trafalgar Square, there was nothing to be done.
>
> (White 1972: 80–2)

Sato's characters have been driven underground by human attention:

> What drove the elves [the Korobokkuru] underground was the violence and avarice of mankind. Outsiders who had heard about the elves tried to catch them, to make money out of them. And they did not come in ones or twos. Sometimes as many as a dozen men invaded the hill. . . . At first they came armed with rakes and landing nets and waved them around blindly. When they realized that they would never catch any elves that way they tried traps and poisons.
>
> (Sato 1988: 92–3)

This in turn forms a parallel with the child protagonists of the 'realist' parts of each of the books since the child protagonists, too, are depicted as similarly vulnerable and suffering. In both books the outer child is constructed in classic-realist mode to simulate the existence of a 'real' person for readers to engage with. There is access to thought-processes, desires, fears, motivation: all designed to make readers feel as if they are sharing an experience with a living human being. The drawing of parallels between the outer-story child and the inner-story images of minute child-like forms draws together the sense of a 'real' outer child of 'now' and the eternal child (expressed symbolically in the sense of the continuity of the communities of manikins and emphasised in frequent references to their 'histories'). Here is a sense of the constant reliving and re-working, over generations, of the experience of powerlessness and vulnerability – the child as victim. Interestingly, White wrote a poem which he titled 'To My Self, Forty Years Ago', exploring the idea of a meeting between his adult and childhood selves in which he addresses the 'child' with both 'pity' and 'reverence'.[29]

Perhaps the most significant *difference* between the two books is in the writers' different modes of controlling access to the story. White's third-person omniscient narrator is interposed between readers and characters in a very 'visible' manner, frequently commenting on events, motivation and the like in a semi-humorous and ironical manner, leaving the words and actions of the characters described to provide the counterpoint to his (technically 'its' rather than 'his', but see below) commentary. Of course, all the characters, including the narrator, are White's creations, but there is a strong sense that the narrator could be interpreted as carrying White's implied authorial storytelling presence into the book (hence my use of 'his').

As with Andersen's presence in his fairytales, White's narratorial self seems to be controlling both the 'realist' outer story and the fairytale inner journey of imagination that begins in the rambling mansion house of Malplaquet and its gardens and wildernesses. Again a poem of White's lends some support for this being an idea that would not be alien to the writer, since in 'Lost' (published in his 1929 collection *Loved Helen and Other Poems*) he specifically uses the metaphor of a large and rambling building with 'corridors' and 'stone stairs' and 'iron banisters' to describe an oppressive feeling of being trapped inside his own thinking. In this sense, White's child protagonist could conceivably be seen as a complex mixing of his ideas of a 'real' child, his metaphorical envisioning of futurity in the form of a child and perhaps, also, an envisioning of his anima image, guiding him into an encounter with his unconscious.

Sato's story is wholly focalised through his first-person narrator, who controls access to every aspect of the tale. Protagonist and narrator are one, even when in retrospective mode the narrator begins his tale with his childhood self and his first encounter with the hill that is home to the Korobokkuru. Throughout there is the sense of this being a deep and quasi-spiritual inner journey for the narrator. Sato's tale follows a quest, begun in childhood, for a secret space, hidden from the outside world, making it possible to see the text as the imagining of an introspective journey, a turning away from the hideous external events of Hiroshima, Nagasaki and the aftermath of war.

Fairytale and 'realist' accounts are mixed in a complicated way by White, since the fantasy part of his text is always treated in a manner-of-fact style, as if it is 'true'. White draws upon Swift's satire, *Gulliver's Travels* . . .,[30] moving forward from the end of Part I ('A Voyage to Lilliput') to create a further fiction which has, as part of its history, an account of the return to Lilliput of Gulliver's rescuer, one Captain John Biddel. White's Lilliputians, as discovered by Maria, his child protagonist, are said to be descendants of Gulliver's Lilliputians.

The writer's tiny 'schoolmaster' (spokesperson for the Lilliputians) claims that, weakened and debilitated by war, 'his' ancestors were captured by the 'normal-sized' human male, Captain John Biddel, and transported across the seas from their devastated homeland. In the Lilliputian schoolmaster's account of this traumatic time in their history, Maria learns that some of the captives died on the way to England, and that the survivors were kept incarcerated in a locked box and taken out to be displayed, periodically, for the amusement of the paying public. In an amplification of the abuse the child Maria endures at the hands of both her governess and the guardian who is embezzling her money, the Lilliputian schoolmaster tells of the abuse his ancestors suffered in the power of their drunken captor and their eventual escape to the hidden depths of the island of Mistress Masham's Repose, located in the heart of a lake on Maria's family estates.

Sato's fairytale miniature creations are also interwoven with the 'realist' aspects of his story, in that the tiny Korobokkuru are treated as if they have a 'true' history, being likely descendants of the tiny god of Japanese folktale 'no bigger than a bean' (Sato 1988: 98), Sukunahikona no Mikoto.[31] The child-self of the protagonist, as outer-story child, is depicted as a 'loner', implicitly traumatised by war. Sato's character/narrator, in whose account suffering and loneliness can be read, is, like Maria, created to give the impression of a 'real' person, creating 'his own' account for readers, filled with apparent access to thoughts, feelings, motivation and the like. The miniature, thus metaphorical, inner-story children (though often portrayed as older in years than the protagonist) finally approach the outer-story child, now a young adult, and ask for his help in safeguarding their hill, a last inner-sanctuary from the surrounding depredations of human violence and greed and the inexorable march of technology.

In each tale, relationships of care between adults and children are highlighted, with young protagonists learning more from the tiny manikins they encounter than from the full-sized adults who interact with them. The books suggest that in this immediate post-war era there is a crisis of belief in the power of adults from the 'real' world to respond ethically to the challenges of coexisting in the aftermath of the evils of what Hobsbawm terms an 'age of catastrophe' (Hobsbawm 1994: 7).

In the 'outer' part of White's book, the 'good' characters, though predominantly well-meaning and kind to Maria, are shown to be either powerless (the Cook) or lapse into forgetfulness or, worse, unethical thoughts of power and self-aggrandisement (the Professor). Although they both offer love and the latter is shown to be capable of giving Maria good advice and as much loving protection as he can, these characters from the 'real' world fall short of the standards set in White's linkage of the inner-story child motif with his envisioning of mothering and the wisdom of elders.

In a critique of the abuse of power, White portrays the Professor as fearing the absolute power he would have over the Lilliputians, were he to encounter them:

> He could not see how beings who were only six inches high could hope to be independent, when they were associated with people who measured as many feet. . . . He agreed with what Gulliver felt among the giants, that it would be better to die than to undergo 'the Disgrace of leaving a Posterity to be kept in Cages like tame Canary Birds'.
>
> (White 1972: 140–1)

Yet, in his desire for the freedom that wealth would give him, the Professor contemplates, at length (the thought processes depicted, as he explores the idea of such an action, occupy nearly five pages of White's book), how he might capture and imprison a Brobdingnagian 'some seventy-two feet high' (White 1972: 141) with the benefit of an aircraft carrier and drugged wine.[32] He even allows himself to speculate briefly on charging 'five shillings for a ticket to see [the Brobdingnagian] having dinner each evening' (White 1972: 145) while keeping an anti-aircraft gun trained on him just in case of any escape attempt.

In contrast, the tiny Lilliputian schoolmaster is very much an image of the wise elder male, offering White's hero, Maria, sage counsel, throughout, in unalloyed fairytale fashion. He is the fairytale counterpart to the Professor, White's flawed 'classic realist' adult male. The schoolmaster is portrayed in story terms as a practical 'father-figure', willing to set aside his books and philosophical ponderings to help Maria learn to relate appropriately to the Lilliputians. He is also depicted as being capable of unselfish bravery in trying to rescue the child from the evil guardians who, at one stage in White's book, imprison Maria in the dungeons of her home. Among other acts of courage, he faces the Cook's (effectively gargantuan) dog, Captain, as he tries to arouse Cook to aid the Lilliputians in the rescue. He is an heroic Lilliputian figure, the enactment of a conjoined father/hero, whose symbolic being is encapsulated in White's vividly absurd, yet poignant, tableau as the manikin offers a minute biscuit to tempt the dog, while his fellows hide behind 'waiting to see how he would fare' (White 1972: 171).

In terms of mothering, although the Cook does her best to care for Maria, bringing her food when she is locked in her room without supper, she can do little when turned away from Maria's door by the governess. In contrast, when Maria picks up a tiny Lilliputian baby, cradled (with possible intertextual reference to Tömmelise) in a walnut shell, only the baby's mother is brave enough to attack Maria:

> There was a fat woman, about five inches high, standing on the marble pavement of the temple, and brandishing a sort of harpoon [the woman has just stabbed Maria in the ankle with this minute weapon.] She was dressed in rust-coloured stuff, like the breast of a robin and she was wild with rage or terror. Her little eyes were flashing, her hair had come down at the back, her bosom was heaving, and she was shouting in an unknown language.
>
> (White 1972: 17–18)

Within the world that White (1972) creates, this is a positive 'dress' for an image of archetypal mothering. Here again the ideal image emphasises the absence of such a figure from the outer narrative, where it is badly needed by the orphaned Maria, who is in the power of a malign adult-female figure, the evil governess, Miss Brown. It is an image of mothering that speaks to the mythic pattern of Demeter as the symbolic bereft mother – an image of mothering that Andersen fails to draw on in his portrayal of Tömmelise's encounters with adult-female figures. Miss Brown, as the opposite of the Lilliputian mother, is portrayed as delighting in cruelty to her orphaned 10-year-old charge. White suggests that this travesty of a care-giver can even contemplate killing the child, as he reveals 'her' inner thoughts:

> if an accident were to happen to Maria? I don't mean any violence of course, not premeditated, but if some little accident did happen, so that she – well – was very ill – or even – even if she died? Quite by accident, naturally.
>
> (White 1972: 152–3)

Moving back to White as implied storyteller, there is an uncomfortable sense that (again a comparable position with Andersen) his female hero may be read, metaphorically, as a young and (here) feisty conjoint appearance of anima/child, ever under threat from the 'shadow' aspect of the female elder in the storyteller's created world.

By contrast, benign maternal influences, focused upon the miniature characters and upon the child protagonist, are vividly present in Sato's book – particularly apparent in the image of the Korobokkuru's tiny and beautiful land, in Sato's evocation of nature in womblike terms, in his image of the lovely camellia tree and in the human form of the old Tomato Lady (wise repository of ancient folklore). Echoing fairytale patterns of the mother-goddess and 'small hero'-son motif of Japanese folklore (see note 31), the miniature people who live inside the later-named Korobokkuru Hill, and later the child protagonist himself, are protected in the womb of the earth. In hero tradition, the manikins venture out, often disguised as tiny frogs (Ishida suggests that the mother-goddess's miniature son is frequently associated with water creatures), and attack predatory men, such as the nurseryman who threatens to uproot the camellia tree, gumming up their eyes and ears and stinging them with 'needles dipped in wasp venom' (Sato 1988: 124).

The small girl-child, Shrimp, first glimpsed emerging from the stream and later hidden in the camellia tree, is depicted in the 'realist' part of the text growing from little child to wise and caring young woman. A positive female figure, she links with the fantasy aspect of Sato's book, bearing all the hallmarks of a princess of fairytale, and could easily be seen as symbolising the protagonist's anima. In a harmony of outer and inner story, she ultimately joins with the male character-narrator to nurture the miniature beings who struggle to survive in their threatened homeland; in story terms she is the protagonist's helper, and, effectively suggested, embodiment of his 'soul-image'.

Sato's adult males, on the other hand, are frequently portrayed as money-obsessed men, those who try to capture and sell the Korobokkuru or officials who care nothing for nature in their plans to destroy fields and places of beauty in their rush to build roads for the lowest possible financial outlay:

> At first all signs indicated that the officials would disregard the villager's petition. Once a decision has been made, officials are loathe to change it merely because some group opposes the plan. Rethinking the highway route would take extra work and extra time. Worst of all, it would cost money.
>
> (Sato 1988: 158–9)

Restoration of a secure and protected habitat is paramount in the 'realist' aspects of both books. In their fairytale subtexts, symbolically, a plurality of manifestations of the divine child (Lilliputians, Korobokkuru) lead, and the simulated-child protagonist of each tale is drawn willingly, eagerly, into experiencing an introspective fantasy world, one that may well arise as metaphorical representation of the unconscious. There is an implicit need, expressed in these books, for the 'children' at their heart to withdraw from the outer world, to undertake an inner journey that is quite unlike the conventional outward motion of the adventuring hero. These children do not venture away from home, they make an inward journey toward rebirth in a 'home' that replaces the inadequacies of their existing lives.

Certainly realist texts for children of the period tend to be, according to Nicholas Tucker, 'child-centred entertainment set in a bland, passionless world where everything eventually falls comfortably into place' (Tucker 1998: 6). Texts that do depict fighting in the 'real' world are of the morally black-and-white adventure genre (such as Captain W. E. Johns' 'Biggles' series). Perhaps outer 'realities' are considered too painful for post-war child readers to bear, or perhaps they are too painful for their writers to engage with. In fantasy texts writers are at least able to allow more painful depictions of conflict to emerge, albeit at a distance from their readers' worlds.

In each of the texts discussed in this chapter, readers are drawn into the shortest of journeys which take them beyond the realm of the 'real' in the sense of a world created with all the semblance of realities external to the text. In White's world, his child protagonist Maria inhabits a crumbling stately mansion in the English countryside; her journey takes her by punt across water to the tiny island of Mistress Masham's Repose, significantly deep *within* her estates:

> She lay face downwards in the punt, looking over the stern into the deep water. Her knees, and most of the front of her were green with slime; the water from the bailing scoop had run up her sleeve. . . . Under her nose, she watched the mare's tail and other flora of the ocean floor, as the prow edged its way between the water lilies. Dragonflies like blue needles, and damsel flies like ruby ones . . . hovered over the surface. By going gently, she could sometimes pass above a flight of perch without disturbing them. Or rather, they would raise their spiky fins, blush out the dark anger of their bars and make mouths at her.
>
> (White 1972: 13)

Reaching the island, Maria's journey to the inner temple takes her through tangled briars and nettles, which scratch and sting as she attempts to penetrate them. At the very heart of this secret place, however, all is still and peaceful:

> Where the brambles ended, the grass began: the same neat artificial grass which Lady Masham must have known. It was still kept as short, or even shorter. It was as smooth as a bowling green.
>
> Indeed, the place was like a bowling green. It was hedged with the thicket, as such greens often are with yew. In the middle, there was the beautiful sun-drenched temple, rising airily on its pillars.

> But what was strange – and here Maria's heart went Pat, she knew not why – the strange thing was that everything was neat.
> (White 1972: 15)

Maria turns her eyes away from her everyday world, from the derelict house of the outer story in which she is maltreated, looks into the depths of an underwater world (perhaps symbolic of this as a metaphorical journey into the unconscious) and then penetrates the brambles that protect the island from outside gaze. White's child figure (perhaps even, at some unconscious level, an envisioning of his anima) is then depicted drawing the storyteller inwards to tell how she penetrates to the superficially serene heart of this mysterious part of her inheritance as she sets out to explore it for the first time.

Besieged in her day-to-day life by the cruel governess, who systematically removes all possessions and pleasures from her charge's life, this inner journey becomes one of growth and maturation as Maria interacts with the tiny people on the island. To her they are smaller than children or pets and completely vulnerable to her comparative size and relative power, yet the majority of the Lilliputians are older and more mature than this (to them) giant creature. White creates an inhospitable, hardly habitable dwelling and shadow-adult figures in his character's outer world and a 'sun-drenched' temple, in the heart of her 'inner' inheritance.

Sato's first person narrator, in a retrospect of his first encounter, as a small child, with Demon's Gate Hill, also penetrates thickets of wild and untamed undergrowth, 'I pushed my way through the branches and bamboo grass that kept slapping into my face' until he stumbles into a hidden clearing, with spring-fed stream:

> I still remember the feeling. I felt as if I had stumbled into a cave. I couldn't help looking up. Yes the sky was up there. . . .
>
> On my right was the high cliff with trees overhanging it. On my left was the thickly wooded slope of the hill. And behind me was the grove of tall cedars from which I had just emerged. These were the three 'walls' enclosing the little flat triangular stretch of ground. Since the cedar grove lay to the south, almost no sunlight reached this mysterious spot. Butterburs, nettles, and ferns grew thickly at my feet. . . .
>
> I noticed a small spring bubbling out of the left-hand corner of the triangle.

> It was the water, clean and quite deep, that first attracted me. The rim around the spring was crumbling in places, but someone had clearly dug it out properly. The skirt of the hill had been shaved straight off, and a deep, dark, little hole dug in its face. Clear water was flowing out of the hole.
>
> (Sato 1988: 11)

Here the secret and dark place described by Sato can be read as a metaphorical representation of the unconscious, particularly associated with maternal images, as in the flow of water from an orifice. In his discussion of 'The Mother Archetype' (*CW* 9i: 156–60) Jung relates 'figurative', non-personal, appearances of the archetype in numinous aspect to a host of images from the natural world, including waters (which can also symbolise the unconscious) and gardens and trees. Sato's description of his protagonist-narrator's first encounter clearly emphasises its 'inner' nature: 'gazing at the spring I forgot all about holly trees. Sunlight filtered through the treetops and gently shimmered on the water. As I moved through the reflected light, I had a dreamlike feeling of having been here before' (Sato 1988: 13).

Sato's hero seems, like White's Maria, to be alone in the world. There is no mention of the protagonist's mother at all, although Sato refers with the utmost brevity to there once being a family (Sato 1988: 36). The father is 'disposed of' starkly in the earlier matter-of-fact mention (see p. 113) of his death and in this single sentence: 'My father was killed in the war' (Sato 1988: 56). Significantly, this rejects the word 'daddy' used in the question that elicits this response: 'Your daddy know about this?' (although it should be noted that this could be the translator's choice of wording and emphasis). The protagonist's birth mother is a conspicuous absence from the text and a nameless father, never described or alluded to, other than in the two brief sentences mentioned above, is killed by Sato, off-stage. The protagonist is identified as an orphan and, effectively, depicted moving inwards to return the womb of the natural world. The movement is emphasised by the allusion to a feeling of déjà vu: 'I had a dreamlike feeling of having been here before' (Sato 1988: 13) and aligns with Samuels' account of Jung's view of the 'incest fantasy', that it is

> not a desire for intercourse with a parent, but a symbolic expression of a longing for the rebirth of oneself through contact with the 'parental soil'. A wholly different meaning for regression

> then emerges: a movement back to a regenerative source for the purposes of personality enhancement and enrichment.
>
> (Samuels 1989: 68)

It is of note that in this introspective piece, perhaps occasioned by prolonged exposure to the ferocities of war and the ultimate nuclear horror (actual and shadow, the latter in the form of the 'Cold War'), Sato's part-'real' part-fantasy world creates a correlation between an inner journey to re-establish connectedness between ideas of 'feminine' and 'masculine' (in partnered images of protagonist/womb, protagonist/rebirth, protagonist/anima) and an outer story in which technology is defeated, hills are not flattened, materialist concerns are harmonised rather than opposed to the natural world (the highway is still to be built, but will accommodate the landscape by going around the hill).

Significantly attached to both the outer and inner worlds the protagonist enters, there are wise elder figures (beyond a personal maternal/paternal) which suggest images of wise old woman and old man – the former, the Tomato Lady, offers the boy an account of the mysteries of Demon's Gate Hill and the latter owns the land there and, ultimately, sells it, in some ways almost hands it down as a legacy, to the young man. The Korobokkuru too have a wise 'Elder' (first introduced by this title on page 86).

Sato seems to draw together 'classic realist' creations of person and place with re-creations of figures from myth and a landscape in which 'real' and fantasy are blurred. The protagonist may link with those readers who respond to the 'classic realist' style of intimate access to the thoughts, feelings and memories of this first-person narrator; but, ultimately they are then sharing a return to the symbolic mother, portrayed as part of the landscape. Here is the image of a regenerative womblike enclosed space; the suggestive lushness of the camellia tree ('red flowers bloomed on the camellia tree [. . . t]hey were a startlingly beautiful color': Sato 1988: 17) and 'the little waterfall tumbling out from the spring' (Sato 1988: 17).

The loss of distancing effected by the presentation of a 'classic realist' character here may stimulate the sharing of Sato's envisioning of a new beginning and growth, as his protagonist, sharing his hopes, fears, loves and dreams with readers, moves from small boy to adult male, finding and joining with his mysterious anima figure; locating and engaging with the 'demons' of the hill; and finally attaining his ultimate goal – possession of this inner kingdom. In

Sato's words: 'On the first Sunday that the hill was mine, it was newly clothed in glistening new leaves. It glowed like a jewel – my own jewel at last' (Sato 1988: 189). This is a powerful suggestion of the attainment of the 'self', in a symbolic encounter with archetypal forms in an inner 'fairytale' landscape.

The realist elements of Sato's story, the location of the fantasy creatures in a relationship with the 'real' characters and 'real' landscape and recorded historical events (albeit linked to the fictional autobiography of the first-person narrator) create parallels between inner and outer worlds. Readers are invited to link with the fictionally created consciousness of the protagonist but, ultimately, as I have suggested, they may be sharing a journey into a symbolic unconscious filled with references to the feminine.

Moving through an outer narrative in which horrors of war, technology and uncaring officialdom are portrayed as evils, the champions depicted arising to defend an ancient peoples are children or young people (the narrator and the female character, Shrimp) and the tiny beings themselves (the Korobokkuru). Victory in terms of the preservation of a natural and untainted environment is achieved by means not of violence but of dreams as the Korobokkuru whisper, nightly, into the ears of those who threaten their land as they sleep, creating dreams and nightmares that warn the sleepers against their planned actions.

The linkage with fairytale worlds and metaphorical expressions of individuation suggests that the outer text may follow the inner harmony of ego and unconscious, thus creating a transcending narrative which encourages readers to imbibe the idea of a new man, appropriately in harmony with the living embodiment of his anima image and reborn from the womb-like natural world – perhaps an 'eco-warrior' with a different idea of 'warrior' – being needed to protect the vulnerable and the land itself.

Sato's tale echoes that of Issun-boshi, in elevating bravery and determination against odds, the effective functioning of male and female, in partnership, in a quest for the fulfilment of their dreams. Unlike the situation in the 'Issun-boshi' fairytale, however, the 'demons' of Demon's Gate Hill turn out to be the tiny Korobokkuru and the battle is with the shadow nature of humankind, as the threatening aspects of the greedy and the materialist predators of the outer world are defused in nightly encounters with the words of tiny children that fill their dreams.

As White's text progresses to a happy ending – the evil characters are taken away to prison; the lands and money are restored to Maria (the Professor's erudition finally proving of value in pursuing her claims); the Professor is elevated to personal tutor (with all that means in terms of not going hungry); and the Lilliputians retain their own kingdom in the heart of Maria's lands. Inconsistencies in the idea of a 'happy ever after' conspicuously remain in the outer story and are, apparently, glossed over. As with the Korobokkuru, who depend eternally on the assistance of an adult human to protect them, so the Lilliputians depend on secrecy and the benign management of Maria's estates, in perpetuity, for their survival.

In the fantasy text, there is a golden end-world. Perhaps Maria as ego-hero confronts and defeats the shadow elders that stand between her and her inheritance. Ego is united with the figures of the unconscious, the encounter metaphorically represented by the protagonist's magical journey to the island of Mistress Masham's Repose and subsequent relationships with its tiny inhabitants. Alternatively, Maria may carry White's anima image, metaphorically guiding the storyteller into an encounter with figures of the unconscious given image as the Lilliputians. There is then a similarly positive outcome in terms of a metaphorical presentation of reconciliation between ego and unconscious. Any transcending communication to readers, drawing together the 'real' and the fantasy of White's creation, perhaps suggests that positive images of wise elder and Demeter-like mothering can still arise in the aftermath of global conflict and inspire the less than perfect, though well-intentioned, figures of the 'real' world to draw together and defeat the seekers for money and power, who abuse the small people they are entrusted with.

Chapter 7

Conclusion

Throughout my case studies I have been looking at the human propensity to give image to the child motif. In particular I have focused on visions of the 'child' arising from the collective unconscious, metaphorically expressed in the image of a manikin. From such beginnings it has been possible to trace ways in which certain archetypal images expressed in fairytale form have been reimagined when viewed through the personal and chrono-topical moment of those who have re-created them as characters for a child audience.

Beyond this, I have looked at the ways such characters are further melded with adult-controlled 'classic realist' simulations of child-alike consciousnesses. Exploring the resulting composite characters, it is clear that many are designed to draw children into their fictional world. They may also, simultaneously, reveal much of their adult creator's ideas about childhood – ideas set into characters embodying guidance, in the form of role models (the desired form of the child) and 'anti-role' models (the feared form of the child) – making plain the conceptions of childness (see note 1) that are current in any personal (whether arising consciously or unconsciously) or chrono-topical moment.

In all the case-study chapters, I have aimed to provide sufficient material from the stories themselves to enable readers to make their own interpretations, which I accept may well differ from my own. As Jung suggests: 'In the last analysis, therefore it is impossible to say what they [contents of an archetypal character] refer to. Every interpretation necessarily remains an "as-if"' (Jung in Jung and Kerényi 1963: 75). I have attempted, however, to draw out what I regard as the salient points in each case-study chapter, but here in my concluding summary I wish to engage, fully, with my own interpretation of what the case-study material may have to 'say' to 'the child that haunts us'.

Why do I speak of the child that haunts us? It is because the inner being of 'child' is always unknown, ever creatively constructed from the outside, though confusingly supplemented, however dimly, by internally-imagined recreations of a time past. Such creations are never truly 'real' and the 'child' remains unreachable (as any psyche that is 'other' to our own will always be), only to be perceived through patterns that are superimposed upon it by adult minds. At the same moment, the 'child' is the very thing adults wish to possess – whether nostalgically, or in the relationships of the 'now', or in order to mould the future. It is just this tantalising (and haunting) phantasm that can enter a potentially flawed alignment with aspects Jung highlights in discussing the child archetype: 'The Archetype as a Link with the Past', 'The Function of the Archetype' and 'The Futurity of the Archetype' (Jung in Jung and Kerényi 1963: 79–83).

Within the unconscious are the seeds for the child archetype to be envisioned in ways that speak to past and future, yet in consciousness the images that arise are continually conflated with adult conceptions of the 'real' child. As Jung emphasises: 'the mythological idea of the child is emphatically not a copy of the empirical child but a *symbol*' yet, in his view, 'lay prejudice is always inclined to identify the child motif with the concrete experience "child," as though the real child were the cause and pre-condition of the existence of the child motif' (Jung in Jung in Kerényi 1963: 80n). But even here one can question what actually constitutes 'the empirical child' or the 'the concrete experience "child"'. Though the terms may appear to refer, quite simply, to multiple physical, living, breathing entities, even here it is essential to avoid use of a reductive 'the' and expand the terms so that they can relate to a plurality. If the inner aspects of such entities are referred to, these are always interpretatively arrived at and anything but 'concrete'. However, fictions produced for a child audience may be a site where it is at least possible to suggest the interaction between symbolic and imagined 'real' and a multiplicity of child readers and readings.

Relating to Part I

Returning to the fairytale image of the child motif, at the base of my study, my summary here draws on Table 2 and is concerned with relating my case studies to the situations and external alliances, modes and conjoined alliances, and tropically-represented aspects listed as relevant to interpretations of appearances of the child motif. In Chapter 2, the fairytale manikins, Tom Thumb and Issun-boshi, are each tropically-represented aspects of the 'child' motif as miniature (metaphorical) child. Their size affirms their powerlessness, yet they are paradoxically empowered, given the magical intervention that relates to their birth and the abilities that allow them to survive, despite fantastical size.

In metaphorical representations of archetypal content in western fairytale, the Tom Thumb image of the child motif appears conjoined with a trickster figure in his adventures prior to reaching the court of King Arthur (and, in some versions, continues in this alliance even while there) and is also the ego-hero of 'his' tale. The character, perhaps in some ways metaphorically representing the genesis of consciousness, is partnered in 'negative' relations with 'devouring' versions of the 'mother' (unconscious) imaged in an aged human birth mother, a cow and a raven and in 'positive' (transformative) relation with a numinous 'great mother' in the form of the Fairy Queen (perhaps envisioned as a 'Marian' figure).

Regarding fairytale as a metaphorical expression of psychic dynamics, in this envisionment the effective anima of this proto-consciousness remains projected onto a 'mother' figure, either the Fairy Queen or, in some versions, the earthly queen (with dire results in *story* terms as the latter situation involves the erotic 'other' becoming entangled with this tabooed mother figure). The 'child's' partnered male figures largely give rise to images of 'positive' relationships and include Merlin and his birth father – who give him visible form through magic and wish – and the King (associated with the Fairy Queen through their gifts). However, the 'child' also encounters 'his' hyperbolic (described as male) 'shadow' self in the forms of the greedy all-consuming giant and the inflated Garagantua.

By contrast, as an archetypal image in Japanese fairytale, Issun-boshi is rarely linked with the trickster figure, and is unmistakeably conjoined with the ego-hero. The character is positively linked with parental and other 'authority' figures (metaphorically, genesis of consciousness is envisioned arising from conjoined mother/father aspects of the unconscious) and, importantly, positively partners anima in the story-form of the Princess 'other' whom 'he' eventually marries. The shadow figures that Issun-boshi contends with (helped by his anima partner) are the hyperbolic oni (gigantic evil spirits). Taking this as metaphorical expression of psychic dynamics, it seems that the tale gives form to a pattern of flowing separation of consciousness from undifferentiated (in terms of female/male aspects) parental figures of the unconscious and an immediate rejoining with the 'feminine' aspects of the unconscious in 'Princess' form. Issun-boshi arises from conjoined 'yinyang' as the 'third' but immediately relates to a (Princess) fourth in a restatement of the symbol. From here, growth of the 'self' is possible, with Issun-boshi enacting a metaphorical envisionment of ego-hero entering the unconscious and meeting and dispelling the aggression of the shadow from within. The '"child" distinguishes itself by deeds which point to the conquest of the dark' (Jung in Jung and Kerényi 1963: 86). Ultimately, growth to full size metaphorically signals a 'growing' into 'wholeness' encompassed through the transformation symbolized in the wielding of the wish-giving mallet.

The fairytale female manikins in Chapter 3 can similarly be analysed using the ideas set out in Table 2. The Scandinavian/western Tömmelise is, in terms of size, again an apparent metaphorical manifestation of the child archetype, however, the 'child' this time is conjoined with Kore (in a re-expression of the Demeter-Persephone myth). The explicit intervention of the storyteller splits the story in two in terms of a metaphorical expression of psychic dynamics (and introduces a personal context).

As ego-hero Tömmelise, venturing on an inner journey, experiences a variety of images of mothering and of 'other' all but one of which are clearly conjoined with shadow. Only the last expression of animus, conjoined with the divine in the 'dress' of the transparently pure tiny king, is purged of 'negatively regarded' sexual energy.

As anima, the tiny girl draws the storyteller deep into confrontation with shadow manifestations both of 'himself' as and of all things maternal. In taking the form of the swallow and fleeing with 'his' anima, the 'dress' of the psychic processes metaphorically represented in the fairytale suggests that the male ego is unable to engage with psychic content relating to male sexuality and aggression and represses all that relates to the 'earthy' maternal sphere.

Regarding both the writer's well-documented personal psychological difficulties (Neil Philip speaks to Andersen's 'conflicted sexuality, his social awkwardness, his hypochondria, his hypersensitivity, his morbid fears'),[33] and the previously identified issues of the repression of sexuality in surface Victorian mores, it seems that this latter pattern has much to do with the 'dress' of Andersen's personal and chrono-topical context. Yet, in many ways, the tale, in both interpretations, robustly restates the tensions that emerge in the western Tom Thumb fairytale. All of which has much to say to the suggestion of a continuing and damaging fear of sexuality and aggression being attached to metaphorical appearances of the child motif, and a pattern emerging of forcible separation of the male child of imagination from the primal maternal, and deliverance to a spiritually controlled and 'pure' domain (whether metaphorically represented by a fairy queen or a fairy heaven).

The interpretation of this pattern is further re-enforced in Ingelow's *Mopsa the Fairy* (with links between 'girl-child' and maiden and the leap from maiden to 'madonna') and in Rossetti's *Goblin Market* (with the repression of the alluring goblin men). However, in the fairytale 'children' of the fairy painting genre, it seems that all that is 'repressed' in the 'dress' of the child (and maiden) motifs of literature comes bursting, explicitly, forth. A. S. Byatt, writing about an exhibition at the Dulwich Picture Gallery, speaks of the latter in the following terms:[34]

> The Victorian fairy painters knew all about the inhumanity of fairies. They inherited a supernatural world from Fuseli's vision of nightmare. . . . His [referring to Richard Dadd] fairies swarm and are all sizes, like Kirk's minutest corpuscles. Their faces are strange, their preoccupations mysterious, their doings dangerous. Joseph Noel Paton painted (as many others did) the quarrel of Oberon and Titania. Some of his fairies are fleshly beauties, and some are gnomes and tiny deformed monstrosities that could have appeared in Bosch.
>
> John Anster Fitzgerald painted a series of sleeping figures – an artist, some young girls – dreaming drugged visions of wraiths, demons and insect-like tormentors. . . . His fairies are not kind. They persecute small creatures, torture snails and robins.

Even allowing for the sensationalist aspects of W. T. Stead's (1885) exposé 'The Maiden Tribute of Modern Babylon' in the *Pall Mall Gazette* (in which he drew attention to the evils of child prostitution, rife in London in the 1880s) there seems to be at least some evidence that the 'dressing' of the child motif in fairy form found expression at a time in which numbers of relatively young children (less than 13 years of age) were being 'sold' into prostitution. Speaking to the idea of 'the little girl as evil incarnate', something she suggests was 'an important part of Victorian ideology', Deborah Gorham (1978), although critiquing Stead's campaign, does put forward the view that the

> confused and conflicting imagery of child prostitution that appears in the rhetoric of the purity reformers of the late-nineteenth century, in which the child prostitute is seen at one moment as a innocent flower and at the next moment [following a single instance of sexual intercourse] as irretrievably and dangerously corrupt, can be related to the contradictions we find when we examine the lives of children and young people of different social classes during this period.
>
> (Gorham 1978: 371–2)

It is just possible that metaphorical images in art form of the powerless/powerful aspects of the child motif, expressed in supernatural 'dress', are somehow entangled in a conflict between the dangerously desired and feared child that arises in some adults' perceptions of the sexual availability of children.

Relating to Part II

In all the fiction examined in Part II there is some form of simulation, though varying in degree, of a 'real' child. The dominant form of the simulated child is that of the idealised and desired model child. The reformed Nils is created as a loving and moral figure and portrayed as being deeply in touch with nature. Arrietty, too, is created as a 'nature' child and a caring companion to the boy and to her parents. Maxie is the epitome of loving 'son' in Kästner's book. White's full-sized Maria, and the narrator-hero of Sato's are, similarly, loving, caring figures, and the latter is explicitly portrayed as another nature-lover; Maria, too, is depicted exploring the natural world around her. In the narratee of 'BB's' books there is another version of the desired child who, it is anticipated, will be sympathetic to the natural world, and filled with an 'innocent' and 'childlike' imagination. Only Cloudberry brings the spectre of the feared child into the character 'cast' of these fictions, and his death seems to 'say' to readers that irresponsibility, boastfulness and deceit lead to a level of egocentricity that has no place in the 'natural' world, where all should work together simply to survive.

For the implied child reader learning of desired (or undesirable) patterns of feeling and behaviour, a web of relationships is established through the simulated child. Adults are predominantly portrayed as villains or mentors and carers (though White and, to a certain extent, Norton, go some way toward creating quite explicitly flawed human mentors). Lagerlöf is alone in eschewing villainy or mentoring attached to human figures, so that the Fox's trickery and death-dealing aggression is attached to a sense of this being a natural phenomenon, as is Akka's wisdom.

Throughout the intra-war and post-war texts there is a distinct suggestion of evil in villains such as 'BB's' Giant Grum, Norton's Mrs Driver, Kästner's sinister Señor Lopez, Bernard and Otto, White's Miss Brown and the Vicar, and Sato's anonymous 'men' who try to trap and kill the Korobokkuru. At a more implicit level, there is a sense of continuity to villainy, and, perhaps more significantly, it is always attached to the exploitation of the miniature metaphorical 'children' of these texts, due to the latter's apparent powerlessness. This seems the feared 'fate' of the idealised child. In Lagerlöf's much earlier twentieth-century work, there is an absence of such specific and directed evil, and the vulnerability of Nils is depicted as the inevitable 'lot' of the hero who must 'naturally' grow and survive (or not – as in the case of Osa's brother Little Mats) through her or his own initiative (as Osa and Nils do) and in acknowledgement that living and dying are matters of fate, though communities (from flocks to families to villages and provinces) can work together to survive and to benefit each other.

Mentors and carers appear in a more mixed pattern. Lagerlöf's Akka and Kästner's Professor are wise and ethically irreproachable, but cannot always be there to protect their charges. In Norton's portrayal of Arrietty's father, Pod, there is much more of a sense of a practical 'human' being (despite his borrower form) who may be right or wrong, but is good at 'heart'. The boy, who inadvertently puts the family in danger but ultimately rescues them, is more a 'child' to Arrietty as older sister. Neither is able to fully protect Arrietty. White's Professor (and possible writer-in-the-text) is portrayed as being self-aware of being flawed and not always able to 'save' Maria. In a reversal the miniature people offer ideal mentoring and caring role models and, far from being powerless because of their size, offer a more effective intervention than surrounding full-sized adult figures. Sato's Tomato Lady and the owner of the hill are much more background figures and not explicitly mentors (perhaps because the first-person narrator is effectively an adult by the time the story is told). Yet the grown-up 'child' is portrayed as mentor to the miniature Korobokkuru in almost (but not quite) 'god-like' fashion, while 'BB's' Pan (with Dodder as acolyte) is an explicit god figure. There is much to suggest that the writers, themselves, desire to protect the 'real' children implied by their simulations, but have been brought to realise or fear that they may be unable to. 'BB's' Pan and Sato's narrator are the only figures that come close to being able to protect their miniature charges in god-like manner.

The simulated children of Part II, however, also arise with an underlying connection to their fairytale counterparts and to the figures that surround these appearances of the child motif. Beginning with the tiny male 'heroes', it is clear that these originate from fairytale male manikins, reimagined in author-created situations and melded with a sense of 'realist' personal identity. These are Lagerlöf's Tummetott (given personal identity as Nils Holgersson), 'BB's' little grey men (given personal identities as Dodder, Baldmoney, Sneezewort and Cloudberry) and Kästner's little man (given personal identity as Maxie Pichelsteiner).

In the hidden psychic processes of the underlying fairytale, Tummetott is the ego-hero of *Nils Holgerssons Underbara Resa Genom Sverige*, but, from the moment he is transformed from 'feared' boy to 'desired' child, any malign sense of conjoined trickster activities is suppressed and 'positive' maternal and anima links are stressed. In other words, the melding of the writer's imaginative child with underlying archetypal potential has resulted in an overturning of many of the patterns of Tom Thumb and creates an image of an inner engagement between divine child, wise mother and anima. The fiction still joins with an underlying fairytale metaphor for individuation, but nature is the new image of 'great mother' and princess anima. The divine child, linked with ideal child, is the architect of the symbolized union between conscious and unconscious. For the writer as storyteller, Tummetott, as animus and the child within, takes her imaging of masculinities from father figure to wise, caring, and brave 'ideal' child as emblem of futurity.

In the short space of time between the publication of Lagerlöf's work and that of 'BB's' gnome stories (a mere thirty-six years) two world wars took place and the world darkened and changed dramatically. Unsurprisingly, the eruption of violence and 'evil' seems to form an implicit and omnipresent backdrop to 'BB's' intra-war and immediate post-war publications. The nearest the gnomes' creator can come to in imagining a conjoint simulated child and image of the child motif brings forward a shadow 'demonic' child to be crushed by a patriarchal god-figure. Here the metaphorical 'child' is linked to the simulated 'negative' role model and the surrounding elderly bachelors, although visually metaphorical children, have no relation to simulated children (seemingly never having been children or fathers, other than in the paternal – in the spectrum of the divine patriarchal – relationships they sometimes enter into with the transient animals and birds they interact with). There seems to be no inner child, only a patriarchal god figure to loom large in 'BB's' text.

The underlying archetypal patterns, exposed in the hidden metaphorical psychic processes of the subtext, bleakly indicate an inner, metaphorical envisionment of a patriarchal ideal, where the eternal child has grown old and lost its symbolic connection with futurity before it is ever young. The subtext seems to suggest a withdrawal from the conscious and regression to immersion in an inner nature/mother/father as the remaining gnomes are drawn into safety over the sea and settle on an island in the midst of a lake. The 'mother' sea is barely recognised in outer story terms, where the explicit link is still with Pan, but 'she' remains as a constant echo under the surface voice of the text as the gnomes gain a new home on 'a green little Island set in a grey, grey loch in the very heart of the blue hills' ('BB' 1988: 255):

> Baldmoney could not speak, his heart was too full. He sat looking first at Dodder, and then at the others and he felt unutterably thankful. In his ears was the low wash of the waves and overhead a star was winking. And as they all stood there . . . each one of them heard another sound above the voice of the sea. . . . It was the Pipes of Pan!
>
> ('BB' 1988: 255)

At a slightly further distance from the Second World War, but still in the era of the 'Cold War', Kästner's (1963) little man, as the dream sequence suggests, must always remain in his tiny form if he is to retain the love of the (father/mother) Professor. In the psychic processes of the underlying fairytale, there seems to be an implicit split between ways of seeing the 'adult' story and the 'child' story. In the 'child' story, child readers may be offered a vision of ego/trickster alliance, identifying themselves with the Tom Thumb-style hero, bravely encountering and outwitting 'shadow' villainy and even preparing to 'taste' the delicious promise of anima. However, there are cross-currents, in that separation from the 'mothering' father is expressed as a nightmarish vision. The underlying story may well speak to an inner vision of suppressed growth and regression to a 'safe' male space, with the figures of the unconscious dominated by a father figure.

In the 'adult' story, the storyteller is aligned with the Professor, holding desperately to an inner bright vision of the eternal child and the 'almost as bright' and desired youthful image of anima. Yet these are figures that speak to potential loss – engagement with anima (though desired and 'delicious') threatens the safety of the little manikin, and the male–male bond.

For the tiny female 'hero' Arrietty, although connections with fairytale are explicitly denied, it is clear that there are elements of the fairytale Tömmelise, and the Demeter-Persephone myth within her. However, unlike the situation pertaining to the male manikins, there is no dual naming and the sense of a 'realist' personal identity is foregrounded – strengthening the feeling that fairytale origins are being suppressed from the surface text.

Looking at possible fairytale patterning and relating this to underlying archetypal content, it seems as if Arrietty as metaphorical child is conjoined (as is Tömmelise) with the figure of the maiden (Kore). Neither Tömmelise nor Mopsa nor Arrietty is envisioned as anything other than specifically maiden, specifically female, though both divine child and Kore partake of the same sense of vulnerability. Indeed, Jung (1963: 158) particularly comments on this aspect of maiden vulnerability and the 'plots' of fairytale are ridden with sacrificial maidens, exposed to devouring monsters and the like. As Tömmelise does, the female manikin imaged in Norton's texts encounters 'shadow' in the form of an evil maternal figure, but 'her' relationship with the overwhelming, but pre-sexual 'boy' brings danger. Only in rebirth (expressed through the symbolic nest) as a natural creature and in a perilous relationship with nature as god-like asexual mother/father is 'wholeness' achieved.

Although the multiple miniatures of White's and Sato's texts are the metaphorical children of the last two books in Part II, it is the full-sized child protagonists that begin the fairytale pattern as the hero myth unfolds and both characters appear to make inward journeys to encounter the child motif (in multiple form) in what appear to be encounters with figures of the unconscious. In White's text the 'inner' expressions of the child motif speak to the kind of ideal envisionment of father and mother in a safe inner haven. In Sato's, the tiny creatures are somehow one with a larger sense of a numinous 'nature' great mother, where the hero is reborn at one with the natural world.

Looking at recurrent themes, strengthened when echoed in both text and subtext, it seems that prior to the cataclysmic events of the early and mid twentieth century, in Lagerlöf's text there is a suggested harmony between female and male, young and old, nature and humankind as these are evidenced in outer lives and images of inner life. By the end of the Second World War, although 'BB's' surface text creates a 'relatedness' with a patriarchal god-figure the subtext speaks to the perceived aridity of inner and outer worlds and perhaps a yearning for an underlying nurturing, female, or at least androgynous, 'great mother'. In Norton's and Sato's subtexts, there seems to be a recurrent sense of the need for rebirth, with again nature as the 'great maternal' of the past, present and future. In Kästner's and White's, there is a paradoxical sense of a need for the inner child to be protected by wise (male) elders, yet a palpable fear that these may fail.

It seems as if the 'child that haunts us' is the child of futurity, the one we periodically fear will not grow according to our desires, the one we periodically fear we can never protect, and the one we ultimately know will move beyond our care. We are, perhaps, obsessed with the child, to the extent that the wise old woman has lost 'her' place in our imaginings and the wise old man is no longer sure of 'his'. Perhaps they will re-emerge in envisionments of nature, as ecological concerns may make us refocus on a search for the source of the primordial child.

Notes

1 Peter Hollindale uses the term 'childness' in *Signs of Childness in Children's Books* (1997), defining it as 'the quality of being a child' and suggesting that it is 'shared ground, though differently experienced and understood, between child and adult' (Hollindale 1997: 47).

2 John Stephens coins the term 'pre-text' in his helpful discussion of intertextuality in relation to children's fiction in *Language and Ideology in Children's Fiction* (Stephens 1992: 84–119).

3 Joseph Appleyard, writing in *Becoming a Reader*, suggests that the 'main reward of reading fictional stories at this age [years 6 to 12] is to satisfy the need to imagine oneself as the central figure who by competence and initiative can solve the problems of a disordered world' (Appleyard 1994: 59).

4 My use of the term 'chrono-topical' returns to a semi-literal idea of a conjunction of time and space (the latter as in topography). It is intended to record a sense of every changing moment, in every changing place, containing and reflecting a unique intersection of the influences of historical time and place, social time and place, and cultural time and place. Although the idea of using chrono-topical may have been suggested to me by Bakhtin's coinage of *chronotope* (as discussed in Bakhtin (1981) *The Dialogic Imagination*), my term is not intended to convey a link with Bakhtin's very specific definition and usage of this term.

5 I am using the term 'fairytale' (following Hull's translation of Märchen) as it is discussed in Jung's essay 'The Phenomenology of the Spirit in Fairytales' (*CW* 9i).

6 Due to the difficulties inherent in fixing the 'real', since our knowledge of the world changes over time, I have used the expression 'the known "possible" world'. This is intended to emphasise that, each time the external material world is considered, what is thought to be possible in it is governed by the knowledge available *at that point in time only*.

7 This is with reference to the Aarne-Thompson classification put forward in Antti Aarne (1999) *The Types of the Folktale: A Classification and Bibliography*, translated and enlarged by Stith Thompson.

8 The 'borrowers' are the central characters in a series of books written by Mary Norton between 1952 and 1982: *The Borrowers* (1952), *The*

Borrowers Afield (1955), *The Borrowers Afloat* (1959), *The Borrowers Aloft* (1961) and *The Borrowers Avenged* (1982).

9 Iona and Peter Opie reproduce this forty-page booklet, printed in London for Thomas Langley in 1621, in *The Classic Fairy Tales* (1974).

10 Rowland (2002: 17), locating Marie-Louise von Franz's work in the field of Jungian studies, suggests that her work is 'characterized by her loyalty to Jung's writings and wishes'.

11 Regarding individuation, Fordham (1953) speaks to the idea of the process as:

> seeking a goal, which eventually define[. . .s] itself as the quest of wholeness – that mysterious entity 'the whole man' – and which necessitate[. . .s] the forging of a link between the conscious and unconscious aspects of the psyche. The experience could also be formulated as the finding of the God within or the full experience of the archetype of the self.
>
> (Fordham 1953: 76)

12 The story is bowdlerised in most later versions produced for children, for example the character is usually depicted as being vomited out of the cow rather than passing through and being released in a 'Cowturd' (Opie and Opie 1974: 38).

13 This, as with all usage of the terms 'feminine' and 'masculine' in this book, is not intended to imply an essentialist connection with bodily sex. It is used here to signify a culturally constructed set of characteristics identified with Jung's use of the terms.

14 I am following Eva Feder Kittay (1987) in her use of the terms 'vehicle' and 'topic' in relation to metaphorical utterances. Kittay draws on I. A. Richards' *The Philosophy of Rhetoric* (1936) in presenting 'vehicle' as the 'idea conveyed by the literal meanings of the words used metaphorically' (Kittay 1987: 16). The second content, i.e. that which the text is speaking about (named the 'tenor' by Richards), is helpfully rechristened the 'topic' by Kittay.

15 In Haugaard's (1994) scholarly translation, *Hans Christian Andersen: The Complete Fairy Tales and Stories*, from whence my quotations from the story come, the name is rendered as Inchelina.

16 H. C. Andersen (1836) *Eventyr, fortalte for Børn*, Volume 2, Copenhagen: Det Kongelige Bibliotek, Nationalbibliotek og Københavns Universitetsbibliotek.

17 The oldest and most complete extant version of the ancient Demeter-Persephone myth is the Homeric hymn 'To Demeter', which is believed to date from the seventh century BC. The Eleusinian mystery religion, of which this myth is the central text, dates back to the Early Mycenaean period (1580–1500 BC).

18 For example in Dag Heede's paper 'Dead women in the work of Hans Christian Andersen', presented at the conference *Hans Christian Andersen: A Celebration and Reappraisal*, British Library, 9 August 2005.

19 See, for example, Lynne Reid Banks' (1981–) ongoing 'Indian in the

Cupboard' series, Raymond Briggs' (1992) *The Man* and Roald Dahl's (1991) *The Minpins*.

20 The implied reader (an alternative way of expressing this is to say the implied reading position) is the *idea* of a reader which is addressed by the implied author of the text. Real 'flesh and blood' readers may or may not respond in quite the way intended, but readers studying the text may well be able to reconstruct both the implied authorial position and the implied reading position, using evidence from the text (see, for example, Chatman 1978).

21 For example, the Opies quote lines relating to the 'pudding' incident (James Field 1611), and reproduce pictures of a woodcut relating to the 'cow' incident (S & J Keys' Edition, Devonport, c.1835), a woodcut relating to the 'raven' incident (Langley 1621) and an illustration relating to the 'giant' incident (illustration by Alfred Crowquill, 1844) (Opie and Opie 1974: 30–40).

22 'One had a cat's face,/One whisked a tail,/One tramped at a rat's pace,/One crawled like a snail,/One like a wombat prowled obtuse and furry,/One like a ratel tumbled hurry skurry' (Rossetti 1939: 12).

23 In Dadd's words:

> On my return from travel, I was roused to a consideration of subjects which I had previously never dreamed of, or thought about, connected with self; and I had such ideas that, had I spoken of them openly, I must, if answered in the world's fashion, have been told I was unreasonable. I concealed, of course, these secret admonitions. I knew not whence they came, although I could not question their propriety, nor could I separate myself from what appeared my fate. My religious opinions varied and do vary from the vulgar; I was inclined to fall in with the views of the ancients, and to regard the substitution of modern ideas thereon as not for the better. These and the like, coupled with an idea of a descent from the Egyptian god Osiris.
>
> (Dadd, quoted in Allderidge (n.d: 22–3), on Demarest (2007) www.noumenal.com/marc/dadd/ (accessed 6 June 2008)

24 A number of Dadd's works and other paintings, such as John Anster Fitzgerald's *The Fairy's Lake*, are viewable on the Tate Gallery website www.tate.org.uk/ (accessed 6 June 2008) via the search facility from that page.

25 In Selma Lagerlöf's speech at the Nobel Banquet at Grand Hôtel, Stockholm, 10 December 1909, she speaks of her 'deep sorrow' that her father is not alive to know of the honour and imagines a conversation with him in Paradise, in which she acknowledges her debt to the 'love of fairy tales and sagas of heroes, the land we live in and all of our human life, in all its wretchedness and glory' (Lagerlöf 1909).

26 Information on Selma Lagerlöf and all those who have been awarded the

Nobel Prize in Literature may be accessed via http://nobelprize.org (accessed 6 June 2008).

27 Tolkien's protagonist in his 1937 tale of *The Hobbit*.

28 In folktale iron is regularly endowed with the power of being able to repel all forms of fairy life (see, for example, Frazer 1957: 225–6).

29 See T. H. White (1929) 'Lost' and 'To Myself 40 Years Ago', in *Loved Helen and Other Poems*, reproduced in full on the website 'England have my Bones': For the Reader of T H White (1996) eds. J. Moulder and M. Schaefer www2.netdoor.com/~moulder/thwhite/lhaop_b.html (accessed 25 November 2007).

30 The full title of the book popularly referred to as *Gulliver's Travels* is *Travels into several Remote Nations of the World by Lemuel Gulliver, first a surgeon, and then a captain of several ships* (Jonathan Swift, first published in 1726).

31 See, for example, Ei'chiro Ishida's (1964) account of Sukuna-hikona no Mikoto in 'Mother-Son Deities', *History of Religions*, 4(1): 30–52.

32 'A Voyage to Brobdingnag' is the second of Gulliver's adventures in Swift's book. In a reversal of the situation when Gulliver is shipwrecked on Lilliput, Gulliver lands on an island where the inhabitants are as big to him as he was to the Lilliputians:

> Undoubtedly philosophers are in the right when they tell us that nothing is great or little otherwise than by comparison. It might have pleased Fortune to let the Lilliputians find some nation where the people were as diminutive with respect to them as they were to me. And who know but that even this prodigious race of mortals might be equally overmatched in some distant part of the world, whereof we have yet no discovery?
>
> (Swift 1902: 94)

33 See '"It's me the story is about": Hans Christian Andersen and the Fairy Tale', paper presented at the conference *Hans Christian Andersen: A Celebration and Reappraisal*, British Library, 9 August 2005. This was briefly available on the internet: www.sas.ac.uk/ies/events/confs/HCA/index.htm (accessed 13 September 2005) (also see Note 18).

34 A. S. Byatt (2007) 'The wild ones', *The Guardian*, 24 November 2007, London: Guardian News and Media Ltd, http://arts.guardian.co.uk/art/visualart/story/0,,2216168,00.html

Bibliography

Primary sources

Andersen, H.C. (1994) 'Inchelina', in *Hans Christian Andersen: The Complete Fairy Tales and Stories*, trans. E. Haugaard, London: Gollancz Children's Paperbacks (this translation first published 1974, trans. from 'Tömmelise', first published 1836).

'BB' (D. J. Watkins-Pitchford) (1978) *The Little Grey Men*, London: Methuen Children's Books (first published 1942).

'BB' (D. J. Watkins-Pitchford) (1988) *The Little Grey Men Go Down the Bright Stream*, London: Methuen Children's Books (first published 1948 as *Down the Bright Stream*).

Coleridge, S. T. (1959) 'Frost at Midnight', in *Selected Poems of Samuel Taylor Coleridge*, ed. J. Reeves, London: Heinemann (first published 1798).

French, F. (1994) *Little Inchkin*, London: Frances Lincoln.

Grimm Brothers (1992) 'Cinderella' and 'Snow White', in *The Complete Fairytales of the Brothers Grimm*, trans. J. Zipes, New York: Bantam.

Hoffman, M. (1986) *The Second-hand Ghost*, London: Marilyn Malin Books in association with André Deutsch.

Ingelow, J. (1912) *Mopsa the Fairy*, London: J. M. Dent and Sons (Everyman's Library no. 619) (first published 1869).

Johnson, R. (1621) *The History of Tom Thumbe, the Little, for his small stature surnamed, King Arthvrs Dwarfe: Whose Life and aduentures containe many strange and wonderfull accidents, published for the delight of merry Time-spenders*, London: Thomas Langley (as reproduced in I. Opie and P. Opie (1974) *The Classic Fairy Tales*, Oxford: Oxford University Press, pp. 33–46).

Kangkang, Z.: see D. Bryant (1989) (Secondary Sources).

Kästner, E. (1975) *The Little Man*, trans. J. Kirkup, Harmondsworth: Puffin (first published 1963 as *Der Kleine Mann*, Zurich: Atrium Verlag).

Lagerlöf, S. (1930) *Further Adventures of Nils*, trans. Velma Swanston Howard, New York: Doubleday, Doran (first published in Sweden 1906–07 – see next entry).

Lagerlöf, S. (1950) *The Wonderful Adventures of Nils*, trans. Velma Swanston Howard, London: J. M. Dent and Sons. (first published in Sweden 1906–7 as *Nils Holgerssons Underbara Resa Genom Sverige* in two volumes with previous entry).

Norton, M. (1983) *The Borrowers Avenged*, Harmondsworth: Penguin (first published 1982).

Norton, M. (1992a) *The Borrowers*, London: J. M. Dent and Sons (first published 1952).

Norton, M. (1992b) *The Borrowers Afield*, London: J. M. Dent and Sons (first published 1955).

Norton, M. (1993a) *The Borrowers Afloat*, London: J. M. Dent and Sons (first published 1959).

Norton, M. (1993b) *The Borrowers Aloft*, London: J. M. Dent and Sons (first published 1961).

Norton, M. (1994) *The Last Borrowers Story: Poor Stainless*, Harmondsworth: Penguin ('Poor Stainless' first published 1966, revised edn published 1971).

Rossetti, C. (1939) *Goblin Market*, London: George G. Harrap (first published 1862).

Sato, S. (1988) *A Little Country No One Knows*, Tokyo: Kodansha (trans. R. McCreery, first published 1959 as *Daremo shiranai chiisa na kuni*).

Sherwood, M. (1977) 'The Story on the Sixth Commandment', in *The History of the Fairchild Family*, London: Garland (facsimile edition from a copy in the Parker Collection in Birmingham Reference Library, London: Hatchard 1818).

Stretton, H. (c. 1878) *Jessica's First Prayer*, London: Religious Tract Society (first published 1867).

Swift, J. (1902) *Gulliver's Travels*, London: Oxford University Press (World's Classics edition) (first published 1726 as *Travels into Several Remote Nations of the World. By Lemuel Gulliver, first a surgeon, and then a captain of several ships*).

White, T. H. (1929) 'Lost' and 'To Myself 40 Years Ago', in *Loved Helen and Other Poems*, London: Chatto & Windus.

White, T. H. (1972) *Mistress Masham's Repose*, Harmondsworth: Penguin (first published 1947).

Wright, J. (c.1700) *The Famous History of Tom Thumb: Wherein is declared his Marvellous Acts of Manhood Full of Wonder and Merriment. Part the Third*, London: Aldermary Church Yard (as reproduced from an original ballad in Ashton 1969).

Zipes, J. (trans.) (1992) *The Complete Fairytales of the Brothers Grimm*, New York: Bantam.

Other fiction mentioned

Banks, L. R. (1981) *The Indian in the Cupboard*
Banks, L. R. (1986) *Return of the Indian*
Banks, L. R. (1989) *The Secret of the Indian*
Banks, L. R. (1993) *The Mystery of the Cupboard*
Barrie, J. M. (1902) *The Little White Bird*
Barrie, J. M. (1911) *Peter and Wendy*
Berry, J. (1988) *Anancy Spiderman*
Briggs, R. (1992) *The Man*
Browne, A. (1981) *Hansel and Gretel*
Clarke, P. (1962) *The Twelve and the Genii*
Cox, P. (1888) *The Brownies: Their Book*
Cresswell, H. (1994) *Polly Thumb*
Dahl, R. (1991) *The Minpins*
Golding, W. (1958) *Lord of the Flies*
Hall, W. (1985) *Return of the Antelope*
Hall, W. (1987) *The Antelope Company at Large*
Kingsley, C. (1863) *The Water-Babies*
MacDonald, G. (1872) *The Princess and the Goblin*
Mitgutsch, A. (illus.) (1985) *The Witch and the Mischievous Seven*
Pratchett, T. (1989) *Truckers*
Pratchett, T. (1990) *Diggers*
Pratchett, T. (1990) *Wings*
Sinclair, U. (1936) *The Gnome-mobile: A Gnice Gnew Gnarrative with Gnonsense, but Gnothing Gnaughty*
White, E. B. (1945) *Stuart Little*
Wrightson, P. (1972) *An Older Kind of Magic*
Wrightson, P. (1973) *The Nargun and the Stars*
Wyndham, J. (1957) *Midwich Cuckoos*

Secondary sources

Aarne, A. (1999) Extract from *The Types of the Folktale: A Classification and Bibliography*, trans. and enlarged by S. Thompson, in M. Tatar (ed.) *The Classic Fairy Tales*, London: Norton (as originally published, Helsinki: Academia Scientiarum Fennica 1964).

Abrams, J. (ed.) (1991) *Reclaiming the Inner Child*, London: HarperCollins (Thorsons).

Annerstedt, C. (1909) 'The Nobel Prize in Literature 1909 Presentation Speech', in H. Frenz (ed. and trans.) (1969) *Nobel Lectures, Literature 1901–1967*, Amsterdam: Elsevier.

Appleyard, J. (1994) *Becoming a Reader: The Experience of Fiction from Childhood to Adulthood*, Cambridge: Cambridge University Press (first published 1991).

Ashton, J. (1969) *Chap-Books of the Eighteenth Century*, Welwyn Garden City: Seven Dials Press (first published 1882).

Attebery, B. (1992) *Strategies of Fantasy*, Bloomington, IN: Indiana University Press.

Bachelard, G. (1964) *The Poetics of Space*, trans. M. Jolas, New York: Orion Press.

Bakhtin, M. (1981) *The Dialogic Imagination: Four Essays by M.M. Bakhtin*, ed. M. Holquist, trans. C. Emerson and M. Holquist, Austin, TX: University of Texas Press.

Baumlin, J., Baumlin T. and Jensen, G. (eds) (2004) *Post-Jungian Criticism: Theory and Practice*, Albany, NY: State University of New York Press.

Bettelheim, B. (1978) *The Uses of Enchantment: The Meanings and Importance of Fairytales*, Harmondsworth: Penguin (first published 1976).

Bryant, D. (1989) 'Making it Happen: Aspects of Narrative Method in Zhang Kangkang's "Northern Lights"', in M. Duke (ed.) *Modern Chinese Women Writers: Critical Appraisals*, New York: M. E. Sharpe.

Byatt, A. S. (2007) 'The wild ones', *The Guardian*, 24 November.

Carpenter, H. and Prichard, M. (1995) *The Oxford Companion to Children's Literature*, Oxford: The Softback Preview by arrangement with Oxford University Press.

Chatman, S. (1978) *Story and Discourse: Narrative Structure in Fiction and Film*, Ithaca, NY: Cornell University Press.

Chester, T. R. (1992) *Trash or Treasure: A Dip into 400 Years of Children's Books*, London: Bethnal Green Museum of Childhood (list of exhibits drawn almost entirely from the Renier Collection of Historic and Contemporary Children's Books, for an exhibition which opened on 28 July 1992).

Clover, C. (1992) *Men, Women and Chainsaws: Gender in the Modern Horror Movie*, London: British Film Institute.

Cox, R. (1996) *Shaping Childhood: Themes of Uncertainty in the History of Adult–Child Relationships*, New York: Routledge.

Dewar, J. (1992) *Law and the Family*, London: Butterworths.

Eekelaar, J. (1991) 'The Importance of Thinking that Children have Rights', in P. Alston, S. Parker and J. Seymour (eds) *Children, Rights and the Law*, Oxford: Oxford University Press.

Fordham, F. (1953) *An Introduction to Jung's Psychology*, Harmondsworth: Penguin.

Frazer, J. G. (1957) *The Golden Bough*, London: Macmillan (first published 1922).

Frenz, H. (ed. and trans.) (1969) *Nobel Lectures, Literature 1901–1967*, Amsterdam: Elsevier.

Gorham, D. (1978) 'The "Maiden Tribute of Modern Babylon" Re-Examined: Child Prostitution and the Idea of Childhood in Late-Victorian England', *Victorian Studies*, 21(3): 353–79.

Haase, D. (1999) 'Yours, Mine, or Ours? Perrault, the Brothers Grimm, and the Ownership of Fairy Tales', in M. Tatar (ed.) *The Classic Fairy Tales*, London: Norton.

Hancock, S. (1999) 'Poetics Plus: Miniature Literature as a Key to Decoding the Structures, Rhetoric and Underlying Topic of Children's Literature', unpublished PhD thesis.

Hancock, S. (2004) 'Jungian Readings of Children's Literature: Animus and Father in *A Wrinkle in Time* (1961) and *The Tombs of Atuan* (1972)', *Harvest: International Journal of Jungian Studies*, 50(2): 61–71.

Hancock, S. (2005) 'Fantasy, Psychology and Feminism: Jungian Readings of Classic British Fantasy Fiction', in K. Reynolds (ed.) *Modern Children's Literature*, Basingstoke: Palgrave Macmillan.

Haugaard, E. C. (trans.) (1994) *Hans Christian Andersen: The Complete Fairy Tales and Stories*, London: Gollancz Children's Paperbacks (this translation first published 1974, originally published 1836 as *Eventyr, fortalte for Børn*, Volume 2, Copenhagen: Det Kongelige Bibliotek, Nationalbibliotek og Københavns Universitetsbibliotek).

Heywood, C. (2001) *A History of Childhood*, Cambridge: Polity Press in association with Blackwell.

Hillman, J. (1983) *Healing Fiction*, Woodstock, CT: Spring.

Hobsbawm, E. (1994) *Age of Extremes: The Short Twentieth Century 1914–1991*, Harmondsworth: Penguin (Michael Joseph).

Hollindale, P. (1997) *Signs of Childness in Children's Books*, Stroud, UK: Thimble Press.

Hunt, P. (2004) *International Companion Encyclopedia of Children's Literature*, New York: Routledge.

Iser, W. (1978) *The Act of Reading: A Theory of Aesthetic Response*, London: Routledge & Kegan Paul.

James, A., Jenks, C. and Prout, A. (1998) *Theorizing Childhood*, Cambridge: Polity Press in association with Blackwell.

Jordan, M. (1992) *Encyclopedia of Gods*, London: Kyle Cathie.

Jung, C. G. (various) *The Collected Works of C. G. Jung* (*CW*), references are, by volume and paragraph, to the Bollingen Series XX, edited by H. Read, M. Fordham and G. Adler, executive editor W. McGuire, trans. R. F. C. Hull, Princeton, NJ: Princeton University Press (unless otherwise indicated).

Jung, C. G. (1990) Volume 9i (as originally selected by Violet S. de Laszlo in *Psyche and Symbol* with updated text to align with *The Collected Works* detailed above).

Jung, C. G. (1991) Volumes 8, 11, 13,18 (as originally selected by Violet S. de Laszlo in *The Basic Writings of C. G. Jung* with updated text to align with *The Collected Works* detailed above).

Jung, C. G. and Kerényi, C. (1963) *Essays on a Science of Mythology*, trans.

R. F. C. Hull, NY: Harper & Row (Harper Torchbook edition) (first published 1941 as *Einfuhrung in das Wesen der Mythologie*).
Kerényi, C. (1931) *The Gods of the Greeks*, London: Thames & Hudson.
Kittay, E. F. (1987) *Metaphor: Its Cognitive Force and Linguistic Structure*, Oxford: Clarendon Press.
Lagerlöf, S. (1909) 'Speech at the Nobel Banquet at Grand Hôtel, Stockholm, December 10, 1909', in H. Frenz (ed. and trans.) (1969) *Nobel Lectures, Literature 1901–1967*, Amsterdam: Elsevier.
Lesnik-Oberstein, K. (1994) *Children's Literature: Criticism and the Fictional Child*, Oxford: Oxford University Press.
Martinez, I. (2004) 'Reading for Psyche: Kate Chopin's *The Awakening*', *Harvest*, 50(2): 105–19.
Nikolajeva, M. (2004) 'Narrative Theory and Children's Literature', in P. Hunt (ed.) *International Companion Encyclopedia of Children's Literature*, New York: Routledge.
Opie, I. and Opie, P. (1974) *The Classic Fairy Tales*, Oxford: Oxford University Press.
Philip, N. (2005) '"It's me the story is about": Hans Christian Andersen and the Fairy Tale', paper presented at the conference *Hans Christian Andersen: A Celebration and Reappraisal*, British Library, 9 August 2005, www.sas.ac.uk/ies/events/confs/HCA/index (accessed 13 September 2005).
Phillpotts, B. (1978) *Fairy Paintings*, London: Ash & Grant.
Pinsent, P. (2005) *The Origins and Development of Children's Literature*, 4th edn, Roehampton, UK: Roehampton University.
Prickett, S. (1979) *Victorian Fantasy*, Falmer, UK: Harvester Press.
Rambelli, F. and Teeuwen, M. (eds) (2002) *Buddhas and Kami in Japan: Honji Suijaku as a Combinatory Paradigm*, London: Routledge.
Reider, N. T. (2003) 'Transformation of the Oni: From the Frightening and Diabolical to the Cute and Sexy', *Asian Folklore Studies*, 62(1): 133–57.
Rose, J. (1984) *The Case of Peter Pan or: The Impossibility of Children's Fiction*, London: The Macmillan Press.
Rowland, S. (1999) *C. G. Jung and Literary Theory: The Challenge from Fiction*, Basingstoke: Palgrave.
Rowland, S. (2002) *Jung: A Feminist Revision*, Cambridge: Polity Press in association with Blackwell.
Rowland, S. (2004) 'Jungian Literary Theory', *The Literary Encyclopedia*, www.litencyc.com/php/stopics.php?rec=true&UID=1508 (accessed 4 November 2004).
Samuels, A. (1986) *Jung and the Post-Jungians*, Hove, UK: Routledge.
Samuels, A. (1989) *The Plural Psyche: Personality, Morality and the Father*, London: Routledge.
Scott Littleton, C. (ed.) (2002) *Mythology: The Illustrated Anthology of World Myth and Storytelling*, London: Duncan Baird.

Skord, V. (1991) *Tales of Tears and Laughter: Short Fiction of Medieval Japan*, Honolulu, HI: University of Hawaii Press.

Stephens, J. (1992) *Language and Ideology in Children's Fiction*, Harlow, UK: Longman.

Tacey, D. (2006) 'The Underground God', in D. Tacey, *How to Read Jung*, London: Norton.

Tatar, M. (1999) *The Classic Fairy Tales*, London: Norton.

Thomas, F. (1994) *Christina Rossetti*, London: Virago.

Thompson, S. (1946) *The Folktale*, New York: Dryden Press.

Tucker, N. (1998) 'Setting the Scene', in K. Reynolds and N. Tucker (eds) *Children's Book Publishing in Britain since 1945*, Aldershot, UK: Scolar Press.

von Franz, M.-L. (1996) *The Interpretation of Fairy Tales*, Boston, MA: Shambhala (first published 1970).

Zipes, J. (trans.) (1992) *The Complete Fairytales of the Brothers Grimm*, New York: Bantam.

Zipes, J. (2000) *The Oxford Companion to Fairy Tales: The Western Fairy Tale Tradition from Medieval to Modern*, Oxford: Oxford University Press.

Web resources

dimadima.com *Little One Inch*, http://dimdima.com/khazana/stories/show_globalstories.asp?q_id=153&q_title=Little+One+Inch&q_country=Japan (accessed 13 September 2006)

Folkloreandmyth.netfirms.com (2003) *Folktales from Japan*, http://Folkloreandmyth.netfirms.com/japan.html (accessed 13 September 2006)

Information Please®. *A Timeline of Recent Worldwide School Shootings*, http://www.infoplease.com/ipa/A0777958.html (accessed 18 July 2007)

Moulder, J. and Schaefer, M. (1996) *'England have my Bones': For the Reader of T H White* (1996) http://www2.netdoor.com/~moulder/thwhite/lhaop_b.html (accessed 25 November 2007)

Quasisemi.com *Issun-boshi*, http://quasisemi.com/myth/i.htm (accessed 13 September 2006)

Index